Nights of Indigo Blue:
A Daisy Muñiz Mystery

Theresa Varela

Pollen Press™

Pollen Press Publishing LLC

2016

Published by Pollen Press Publishing LLC
PO Box 1572
Radio City Station
New York, NY 10101-1572
pollenpress.com

Printed in the USA
Edited by LaShawn Pagán
Cover Photo and Art Design by Patricia Dornelles

Copyright © Theresa Varela
All rights reserved
Originally published by Aignos Publishing, Inc., in 2015

Library of Congress Control Number: 2016917218
CreateSpace Independent Publishing Platform, North Charleston, SC

13-digit ISBN: 978-1539071815
10-digit ISBN: 1539071812

All rights reserved. No part of this publication may be stored in a retrieval system, transmitted or reproduced in any way without prior agreement and written permission of the publisher. This book is fictional; no character portrayed in this story is intended to be based on or having originated on any actual living person known by the author or any individual involved in the publishing of this novel. The author and publisher have neither liability nor responsibility to any person or entity with respect to any loss or damage caused, or alleged to have been caused, directly or indirectly, by the information conveyed in this book.

For Patricia Dornelles…
for encouraging me to walk through new doors

Author's note

I've often heard that an author should write the story that they would like to read. This is what I've done here. I'm an old school mystery lover, my mother shared her affection of Agatha Christie's and made sure I had my never ending supply of Nancy Drew and Cherry Ames novels. These books intrigued me and colored my vision of people, the world, and all the intricacies involved. One missing element in those mysteries was that most of the characters and storylines had very little to do with me.

I grew up in the Park Slope, Brooklyn, NY, that now seems to be a myth. Back then, the neighborhood was still affordable and open enough for the masses to claim apartments, restaurants were cuchifrito joints, Salsa music swelled from windows, and kids played skellsies on their knees daring cars to glide by, or danced in front of fire hydrants without sprinkler caps on to protect their tender skins, while parents looked on from their brownstone stoops. This is the historical backdrop of my life, and therefore, while I may never specifically write these details in my stories, they are there and can be heard in the rhythm of my storytelling.

The characters in *Nights of Indigo Blue* represent lives that are familiar to me. I wanted to write a novel that spoke freely of misas, spiritual séances, dark pasts, the depths of friendships, and the transcendent love between people. There's a little of my protagonist, Daisy Muñiz, in all of us- inspired, awkward, honest, open, and willing to do what it takes, even when it's a tad uncomfortable to make a change. I hadn't found a mystery that I could relate to that was close to my experience in this particular universe at this time, so I figured it was up to me to write it. Creating a mystery made it all the more fun.

When there's a need out there in this great big world, and I can do something to fulfill it, I will. That's a charge for me this lifetime and as an author, I strive to write about the power of mundane worlds because that's what I believe we live in and it's up to us as individuals to make the magic if we haven't found it already. I applaud those of us who allow the ordinary to become extraordinary. So, read on lovers of the implicate and explicate orders of our Universe… it's all in the story…

I'd like to thank my editor, LaShawn Pagán for her efforts into making this book what I envisioned and for her raucous laughter during line edits.

-Theresa

Chapter 1

Swallowing my pride was the first step I took when I agreed to work on Saturday. It was bad enough that everyone knew me, but the fact I'd been promoted and still had to work extra time was embarrassing. It had been a while since I worked at the weekend out-patient clinic. Saturdays were dedicated to cosmetic surgeries. Easy enough and the money came in handy. I had to admit that it made me feel good when the supervisor asked me to help out. I guess my skills as a clerk were more important than my history. I didn't want to think about that. My plan was to keep my focus on paying off my last three credit cards.

"So, have you missed me?" I buttoned up my gold colored smock. "A bunch of people getting their noses and chins done, huh? They must be getting ready for the holidays," I said jokingly to Allie while standing at the reception area desk that gave me a bird's eye view of the people who were coming in for a bit of surgical sprucing up. A nose realignment, a tummy tuck, or a breast or butt shape up could do wonders for the soul. If they didn't get what they wanted for Christmas it wouldn't sting so hard when they gazed at themselves in their mirrors.

"Of course, we missed you, Daisy. Glad you could help out today. It's been a real zoo here." Allie rolled her eyes. She was an old friend from my not-to-be-celebrated past. I didn't have that many of those friends left over these days. "We're a couple of months away but that gives enough time for the swelling to go down. These folks will look splendid just in time for Thanksgiving. Here, have a look at this schedule." She handed me the list of Saturday morning surgeries.

"Not that you asked, but I've missed you too." I smiled at her. She was all right. I liked her even though she was now more of a work buddy than a friend since I stopped meeting her at the Blarney Rose across from the hospital. That place gave me a headache. "I can't believe I'm back for Sixth Saturday."

On every sixth weekend the usually quiet operating rooms came alive for people who were either unable or unwilling to take a day during the week to address their cosmetic concerns. The reception lounge was filled with people awaiting their early morning reconstructive surgeries. The lounge area was almost as plain as the people who sat in it. The walls were papered a sea green with brown trimming to accent the brown leather seats. A few large lavender colored faux floral arrangements dotted the area. Enormous vases holding fresh flower arrangements that had been donated by wealthy and happy clients were also scattered about the room.

None of the pre-operative clients had eaten since midnight. Hardly anyone was talking. Some paced the room while a few others listlessly scanned old copies of GOLF magazine. Everyone was responsible enough to bring a suggested escort in with them, that person was intended to accompany their drowsy and pain ridden bodies home at the end of the day. The escorts, with their full bellies, were the ones who attempted to chat and were answered by the grunts of hungry patients waiting to be called in. Like always there was a rebellious one, who against all rules, had brought in a Styrofoam cup that filled the air with the aroma of toasted coffee beans, disturbing those who cared enough to follow medical instructions and stopped eating from at least midnight the prior evening. Their discomfort was obvious in their eyes as they glared toward the cup every time it was raised towards the lips of the lone rebel slowly sipping the delicious black liquid.

Allie pointed to the day's list of scheduled surgeries. "Look, Garden Stills and Mrs. Jacques are back."

"I think they have surgeries because they're bored." I shook my head. "These women are unbelievable. They have too much time on their hands and end up standing in front of mirrors all day."

"Lots of money to burn, if you ask me." Allie was pensive. "So, tell me, why are you here? Slumming?"

I was shocked. "I can't believe you said that! No, I'm here to pay up some of those credit cards. You know, finish them off. I'd like to receive junk mail only, if at all possible. Here, give me those sheets. I'll get the labels on them for you."

Allie laughed. "Tell me about it. I have a pile of bills that I just keep stacking up until they fall over. Then I have no choice but to open them up. I worked the O.R. a couple of days last week. It's funny how when they float me over to O.R., I don't want to go, but if it's an extra shift, a little more cash, I'm on it."

"Being a nurse definitely has its perks," I said. "You can work so many different units. I remember how irritated you'd get every time Kay told you that you had to float. I wonder how she's doing now."

"The last I heard she was having a grand old time in Florida." Allie made a face. "She inherited her mother's condo and retired."

"I didn't realize that she was ready for retirement." I started printing out copies of advance directives that the clients would be signing throughout the day. "Good for her."

Allie shook her head and shivered. "Living in a house someone died in is not my idea of a good time at all."

"It's just not anyone really, it was her parent," I

said, pushing my hair out of my eyes. It was getting too long and too thick, and I remembered for a quick moment that I needed a trim. Maybe I would add some red highlights to go in with the rich brown tones. "Anyway, it's not really scary."

Allie pointed with her chin at the sea of faces sitting in the large waiting room. "I think we should start calling the first one pretty soon. They look terrified." She shook her head. "I've been a surgical nurse most of my career but I can never get over how this group always looks so unhealthy even though they're coming in for elective surgery."

"No make-up, no food. Besides, who's going to have their hair done just to have it smushed under a paper cap?" I tried to keep my laughter low. "It's six in the morning, we're indoors. It's not a great place for sunglasses. Those are usually a saving grace."

Allie looked distracted for a moment when the double doors to the operating suite swung open. A couple of laboratory technicians strolled in and she went back to the list in her hand.

"Disappointed?" Something was up. I could feel it.

"Me? Disappointed? Why would you say that?"

"Because I've worn that look plenty of times, but, hey, it's none of my business. I'll have these ready for you in a jiffy." I piled the instruction sheets and consent forms together. "I have to say that this is mind-numbing. I don't miss being a ward clerk anymore."

"So, how has it been working for Sophia?" Allie asked. "How long have you been with her now?"

"It's been almost a year. Did you know that she just got promoted to Administrator?" I stapled forms together. "Do we need more living wills?"

"Yes, they're on that shelf over there. The new

manager had us move everything around. Where does Sophia's promotion leave you?"

"I'm still her assistant but now I have a better office, with a view. Granted it's over the parking lot but I do like the sun coming in during the afternoons."

"I'm glad you made it out of the units. You can lose your life working in them." Allie caught me watching her. "Don't feel sorry for me. This is fine. I don't have to think too much, just do, and my shift is over."

"Do you see any of the old gang? The one thing I miss is the joking around. There's none of that around Sophia, she's always got her eye on me."

"Can't blame her, can you?" Allie's voice lowered to a whisper. "She's known you for years."

"I'm a different person now. You wouldn't believe how different." I shrugged. "But, tell me, do you ever see what's his name… John McDeevers?"

"I heard that he's over at Lutheran now. He's a radiologist. He grew up too."

"Don't remind me! What a group. What about Doctor Campbell?"

"Doctor Campbell?" Allie picked up a couple of the forms. Clearly, she was ready to start her admissions process.

"Yes, I heard he got married. Is that true? He was last of the great bachelors. I can't believe it."

"He's just back from vacation, actually from his honeymoon." Allie pulled the blood pressure cuff toward her as she readied to call the first client into pre-op cubicle number one. "Where is that nurse's aide? She's supposed to be here taking vitals."

"She's around. Don't worry about it. You know that this place practically runs itself." I thought about him for a moment. "Amazing… he was such a playboy."

"You're still on him? Playboy or boy toy, it depends on how you look at it. I heard that his wedding was gorgeous; some of the interns were talking about it the other day. I wouldn't doubt that it was lovely. He married Doctor Price."

"Are you serious? The ice princess, oops, I mean the chief surgical resident?"

"You got that right." Allie sighed. "They say that her dress was absolutely stunning. Ivory... one of the interns said that it was divine."

"How did she ever warm up enough to get involved with him? Although, when it came to girlfriends he wasn't the choosy type." I wiggled the bare third finger of my left hand. "I never thought Doctor C. would commit to anyone. Wonder why he finally decided to hitch up after being divorced after all those years without anyone hanging on."

"I don't know but, right now, we've got to get back to reality. There's plenty to do here. We don't have time to wonder about Doctor Campbell's love life." Allie flipped her ponytail over her shoulder. "I have to make sure that the new aide checks those vitals and documents them correctly, otherwise I'll never stop hearing it from that supervisor. She's always on my case for some reason."

I stacked the readied documents in front of Allie on the admission's counter and gave her a thumbs up. "Ready to start whenever you are. We'll have plenty of time to talk later anyway, once we get through the mad morning rush. The afternoons are always lighter. You know these docs; they all want to be first on the schedule."

The surgeons were known to schedule their surgeries as early as possible for the Operating Room. They had surgical rounds, classes to teach, residents to supervise, suits to buy, and wives to placate for the hours that they spent in their mistresses' beds, in addition to time spent at their clients' bedsides.

I called the first client over to register for her surgery. "Hi, I'm Daisy Muñiz. I'm going to ask you a few questions. Get you in as soon as possible for your rhinoplasty." It wouldn't do for me to call it what it was- a nose job.

The admissions desk was a center zone of organized chaos. Why the doctors didn't deal with advanced directives and living wills in their offices before the day of surgery was beyond me. Instead, here I was, me, someone they didn't know from a hole in the wall asking them whether they wanted to be put on life support in the event something bad happened. So many people had no idea what sort of medical treatment they wanted in the event they were unable to voice their needs in case of an emergency.

I flashed back to when my boyfriend, Lou, had been on a ventilator after the accident. I'd been his unofficial next of kin until the doctors needed the real thing, official, before he died. Watching his relatives' make life and death choices for him was excruciating for me. The fact we lived together for a few years didn't seem to count at all. Even though we hadn't actually talked about what our decisions would be beforehand, I knew his desires a lot better than his mother and aunts… a little too well. My stomach lurched and I knew I had to concentrate on today and not get caught up in my thinking about those awful times.

The shift flew by with the help of a tight highly-skilled team of nurses and patient care aides. Each client had come in with a purpose- to have their surgery, recover, and return home. I missed this since I began working as

Sophia Cornelius' assistant. I was entirely responsible for making sure that her ship navigated through any course without sinking. Making amends to my credit card companies had me watching my debt decrease and my credit score increase but I also loved working with my old friends in a safe place, far from bars, and the crazy clubs that we'd hung out at not that long ago. They still hung out. I'd had to say good night for a bunch of reasons, my debt being only one of them. Blowing up the A.T.M.'s on Friday nights had become a specialty.

"It wasn't a bad day all in all." I reviewed the pre-op list. "Did you see this? Doctor Campbell is actually scheduled as being on today? Funny, we were talking about him just this morning."

"Doctor Hagar switched with him- something about rescheduling because of the honeymoon. He did him the favor at that point and now, well, you get it..."

"Why didn't you say something earlier? We weren't that busy today. We could've said hi, congratulate him or something."

"It didn't occur to me. A few of these clients made the day harder than it needed to be," Allie said. "Some of them get so much surgery; they act like they should have special treatment. It's as though they believe they should get a gold card or something."

"Really, was today that awful?" I asked.

"Not everyone, just a select few."

"What's eating you? I didn't realize that anyone gave you such a hard time today," I said. "Want to talk about it?" Allie was always like that. She kept her feelings in and no one ever really knew what was going on with her. I don't know how I forgot that in such a few short months. Like they said in the rooms, I had a built-in forgetter.

Allie bristled. "It's just that a couple of the clients

think they own you. It's a status symbol or something. If you can get liposuction for your knees…"

"Hey, I'm surprised, I never heard you talk like this before." I tried to calm her by putting my hand on her shoulder.

"Never mind me," Allie apologized. "Forget it. I'm sorry. I'm probably hungry."

"Don't worry about it. I'm sure that nobody can hear you but you need to be careful, you could get written up for talking like that around here."

"Listen to you… you have changed."

I tried to lighten the mood. "I guess I've been working around Sophia a little too long. She must be rubbing off on me. Don't let her know otherwise…"

The double doors to the operating area flew open. One of the nurses, capped and dressed in scrubs, gave me the high sign: time to call a code. One of the patients must have stopped breathing or a heart monitor showed someone was about to flatline. The staff could never take for granted how risky surgery could be even if it was a routine nip and tuck affair.

"Recovery Room!" She pointed at Allie. "We need you back here!"

Allie ran into the recovery room and the doors automatically closed behind her. It was late and most of the staff had already left for the day.

I picked up the phone to have the operator page the code that indicated a patient had stopped breathing. "Code 99 to the Recovery Room."

I waited for further instructions. They'd probably need me to print out labels for blood gases or other laboratory specimens. If the Respiratory Therapist didn't get there quickly enough, I knew to call them back. The tinny sound of the operator's voice on the overhead loudspeaker called, "CODE 99 to the Recovery Room!" A few residents, interns, and the respiratory therapist pushing equipment ran past me in through the double doors. Everyone had arrived. I wouldn't have to call twice.

Allie returned to the desk a few minutes later. "False alarm. No code. Doctor Campbell was there with the nurse. There was a problem with Mrs. Stills. She had an episode of hypotension. You can cancel the code. They're going to transfer her to Intensive Care just to keep a close watch but I'm sure she'll be okay."

"That's a relief." I watched as most of the staff that had just arrived filed out through the front entrance. "You look tired. Do you want to go out for a bite?"

"Dinner sounds like a good idea," Allie said, yawning widely. "I'm tired but I have to eat. Just wait for me to go to the locker room. I've got to change, be right back."

"Take your time. I'll be sitting right here." I dug deep into my bag and pulled out my diamond cut steel nail file. There wouldn't be any one around at this time of day. No one would make any rude comments about me filing my nails. The cuticle of my left index finger had been catching onto the paper work all day. My nails were uneven and my cuticles were jagged. They were awful, so I went to work on them. There would be less for the manicurist to do if I ever got back to the nail salon.

"Miss!"

I jumped at the voice that broke me away from the subtle scratching sound of metal against my nail. Banging into a small vase of coral colored carnations, I watched the water spill across the counter top and onto my favorite silk gray pants. Although most of my clothes were my favorite these beauties really were my favorite: I'd gotten them on sale for $99.99.

"Miss, can you tell me where I can find Doctor Campbell?" The face behind the hoarse whisper was that of an enchanting leprechaun. If she hadn't been wearing green, it might have been the voice of a wood sprite. Whoever it was, I was dazzled. The woman's short brown hair curled around earlobes that held tiny gold spheres. Her large blue eyes were framed in dark lashes. Was she for real or had I been reading too many fairy books in my quest for 'spirit?' I could practically hear my best friend, Jose, saying, "Daisy, back to earth, Daisy, back to earth."

"I'm sorry..." I grabbed a couple of napkins and made an attempt to sop up the water that was quickly seeping across the counter of the nurses' station.

"No, I'm the one who's sorry, did I do that?" she asked. She looked young and had a thick Irish brogue. Not your everyday occurrence in Brooklyn. "I didn't mean to startle you. Here, let me get that." She grabbed the napkins and began wiping up the counter top.

"Just a minute, I'll get more paper. Be right back," I said, before running to the visitors' bathroom located right next to the entrance of the lounge. I picked up a wad of paper towels and hurried back. When I got there I saw that the pixie lady had already left. I cleaned up the station and tried to salvage my sweet silks.

"Ready?" Allie returned wearing jeans and a floral top. She pulled on a form fitting brown suede jacket and bent down to place her pant hems over her ankle cut boots. She took one look at me wiping up the mess my pants had become and asked, "What happened to you?"

"Wherever I go, I seem to spill water at some point or other. But this time it wasn't my fault. Never mind... it's a long story... let's go. The pants will eventually dry."

"If it's okay with you then, I'm ready to get out of here."

Allie looked very different than the woman who'd been in hospital attire all day; very sophisticated. Her hair was long and she had natural auburn mixed in with a deep natural black that made her hair look like dark silk reflecting the red of an evening sky. She said it was the result of having an Irish father and a Taina mother. The mixture made her naturally gorgeous with a nose and cheekbones that were to die for. There were no photographs in the surgical reconstructions binder that showed human ability to recreate such beauty.

"Good thing I have some self-esteem here," I said. "Allie, you look fantabulous. Did you ever think about modeling instead of nursing?"

"Yeah, right." Allie winced. "Me? Model? I don't think so." She placed her folded scrubs in her bag. "These need a good wash so I'd better get them home."

I took my dripping smock off. It hadn't helped keep me one bit dry. "I'm just going to throw these in the laundry bin. I don't know why you don't do the same. Let the hospital take care of it."

We went through the double doors to the suite. The place was practically empty. Only a couple of staff and clients were still there. Waiting for the elevator we watched the maintenance man, Jimmy, as he buffed the already shiny tile floor. The usual frenetic energy seemed to calm down with the hum of the machine. The elevator doors opened.

"Have a good night!" I called out as we went inside. It was nice seeing Jimmy. Some things never seemed to change.

"Good night!" he answered without looking up.

❀

We finally stood in front of the tavern located right

across the street from the medical center. This was one of our old hangouts and it seemed like forever since we'd been here. I could feel the familiar craving in the back of my mouth. We went in and sat down. I knew what to do. I'd practiced a lot these past few months, relearning what I knew.

"I'll have an iced tea." I ordered as soon as I could get the server's eye. She knew me a little too well.

"No beer, Daisy?" She seemed surprised.

"No, I'll have the iced tea and a burger."

"Me, too," Allie chimed in.

I was surprised this time. Allie had been my running buddy, but I knew better than to make a big deal about it. I watched the server go over to the bartender. He raised his eyebrows as he rinse-wiped off the bar counter top. I decided that I'd focus on looking forward to a charcoal broiled burger.

"How is it for you being back?" Allie asked. We'd been thick as thieves before I put down my last glass of wine... or was it a bottle of beer? That was something that still disturbed me. I couldn't remember my last drink. It was still a blur. My sponsor, Angela, told me that my memory would probably come back. So far it hadn't.

"I'm good." I really didn't want to go down memory lane. It might not have been the best idea to return to the scene of the crime. "I'm more tired than I thought. How about we eat fast? I need to hit the sack."

Allie nodded. We chatted about the goings on at Windsor Medical Center. We worked at the busy Park Slope hospital for a few years and knew most of the old timers. Crazy as it seemed, I'd probably be considered an old timer myself. It felt weird to be at the tavern with Allie and I was glad when we said our good nights. I hugged her and then we went our separate ways. She wasn't to blame for my inadequate feelings; they all had to do with me. I was the one who felt like I was walking through a minefield just because I'd chosen, yet again, to step foot into a bar.

I walked the few short blocks to my house. The almost full yellow moon smiled down at me as I made it to the old brownstone. There wasn't a soul out on the usually busy street. Gas lamps flickered in the fronts of the regal line of homes. The neighborhood had become mine and I loved it.

Looking up at the bay window of my bedroom, I steeled myself for another night alone. Dinner with Allie hadn't done much to make me feel better. It reminded me of the stark differences in my life and the changes that had seemed to swoop down from nowhere. I knew that wasn't really true. If I wanted, I could point exactly to the place where I made decisive choices resulting in this bored façade of a life- a life that seemed to yawn just like the windows of the house. The moon had no business smiling. I grabbed the bannister and dragged myself up the stairs to my apartment.

Chapter 2

A good night sleep always helped. The trouble was that they were hard to come by. I spent more time looking at the walls of my newly decorated apartment than I wanted. My bedroom had become more of a meditation center than a sleeping cove. Loving the apartment was one thing but staring at the palest pink hued walls at three in the morning was something I hadn't planned on doing when I chose the color. Fortunately, I'd gotten to sleep last night with Ms. G., the black and white fur ball lying at my feet. My landlord, who lived on the first two floors of the brownstone, had to admit that I was her kitty's favorite tenant of all time. Stretching my arms and legs out as far as I could, I felt a tingle go down my spine. Something was up. I wasn't sure what exactly it was but I'd been practicing listening to my personal intuitive signs. I was trying to be completely aware of my body and what was going on. It was almost like pulling a daily morning tarot card. At some point during the day I'd usually get a clear sign as to what the tingling meant.

I felt refreshed for a Sunday morning and decided to go to a meeting. I heard often enough that 'meeting makers make it.' I wanted to make it desperately. In the past, mornings had been me waking up to half filled glasses and bottles next to my bed and it would take hours for me to shake the fuzz on my brain loose.

The shower water was freezing, I sort of half hugged and half soaped myself, in a hurry. I wanted to get to the 10 a.m. meeting at St. Augustine's basement around the corner. A few minutes later, I'd thrown on my rattiest jeans and a long sleeved tee-shirt. I pulled on a pair of ballet flats and moved toward the staircase. They didn't really feel good but looked good. Too flat for my high arches but they made my ensemble of shabby chic perfect. I started down the stairs. Since I'd had to work on Saturday, Sunday was the day I looked forward to. Any day could be a relaxation day. No need to get anxious because half of my weekend was already gone.

"Hey, look who's here." Jose peeked up at me from the third floor landing. He shared the apartment below me with his longtime partner and love, Rubio. Jose was dressed in a white tunic slung over white jeans. His small embroidered white skull cap covered his dark curly brown hair.

I practically squealed when I saw his whole outfit. "You're a sight, look at you! I don't think I'll get used to seeing you dressed like this."

"I'm halfway through my year so you'd better get used to it." Jose was in his first year as an initiated priest of Obatalá in the Orisha tradition. "What are you doing up so early on a Sunday morning?"

"I have to make a meeting. I slept last night but it was me- alone. No meetings the last couple of days. I want to start the day off right. I refuse to be like a bear rattling around in a small cage. That would not be a good thing."

"Wait for me, I'll go with you."

"Where were you going?" I checked him out closely. "You're up mighty early yourself."

"To throw out the garbage?" Jose looked sheepish as he held out a small half-filled black plastic trash bag.

"On a Sunday morning? Yeah, right. Something's up," I said. "Hurry up, I'll wait for you. The meeting starts at ten."

Walking toward the turn of the century Church a few minutes later, Jose sighed. "Rubio didn't come home last night."

"Are you kidding? Out all night, since when?"

As far as I knew, Jose and Rubio were the golden couple- together since their first year of college. They'd weathered lots of storms together but infidelity had never been one of them. I decided not to be so negative.

"I'm sure there's a reason. Did he at least call?"

"This is the second time since I've been stuck in the world of iyawó-dom. No going out after dark for me. No eating at restaurants. He's not the one who's been crowned. It's been rough... and no, he didn't call."

"I'm surprised," I said. "He's crowned and he knows all about it. I thought he was supportive of your decision."

"He was... is." Jose gazed up at the large trees whose leaves were like festoons of gold and reds. A couple walking their chocolate Labrador passed us. "I was shocked the first time he stayed out. His excuse was that he had a late meeting with the owner of a gallery for the show next April. He said he was in a large group and they all ended up at some dude's house in Jersey... a midnight pool party that ended at sunrise."

"Well, no one's diving into a pool now, it's October." I could barely conceal my annoyance.

"Try not to be upset. He doesn't have a gallery. He's dependent on these folks. It's a transition... my life's changed. We'll get through it. I love him and know that he loves me. The most important thing is that I trust him."

"If you say so." I tried to shake off my feelings to support my friend. It seemed like I was doing an awful lot of that lately.

We came to a halt in front of the massive brownstone church and made our way down the basement stairs. After grabbing cups of coffee at the table at the back of the meeting room, we settled in for the next hour. I'd been sober for almost a year, thanks to the help I received from Jose. Because of his white clothing, he seemed like a beacon of light in the otherwise dark room. We listened to the speaker as he shared about his experiences, often laughing, even though much of what he said, in actuality, was tragic. Neither of us shared our thoughts after the speaker ended, but listened to some of the others who shared about their experiences and the reasons they decided on living alcohol free lives.

After the meeting and greeting a few of the others, we left the poorly lit stairwell and were now on the busy street. Jose looked down at me and smiled. "You saved my life today."

"Glad to be of service," I said, "because you saved my life almost a year ago." I swung my arm around him giving him a hug that lasted a few moments. Jose had twelve-stepped me into sobriety just as I was about to fall headlong into an abyss of disaster. I hadn't realized that a glass of wine could play such havoc with my life until Jose had shared his own story with me one afternoon. It took me a while to get what he was talking about, but I finally did.

"Let's go to my place for breakfast." Jose looped his arm into mine. "I can't eat at a restaurant but I can make a mean plate of bacon and eggs."

"Bacon and eggs?" I pretended I wasn't interested by a quick crinkle of my nose.

"Okay, home fries too."

"You're on!" I laughed. The dark loneliness of the previous night was finally and completely gone.

※

I sat at the Formica table in their tiny kitchen. "These are great, aren't they?" I chewed one of the sweet rolls we'd picked up from the bakery. The television droned on in its corner on the counter.

"Tell me, are you going on a trip or something?" Jose took a sip of some coffee waiting for me to answer.

"No. I had hoped to go to Puerto Rico for a work conference in Rincón. But because the hospital is tightening its belt I don't get to go. The C.E.O. wants his secretary to go and she'll handle everything."

"I wouldn't give up yet."

"It's not something I can choose. It's disappointing but they've already made the choice on who is going. I really had hoped to go. I have family there that I haven't seen in about a hundred years."

"What are you? Twenty something? A hundred years!" He looked at me again. "Something tells me you might be going anyway. Keep some of your summer clothes out and ready to pack."

"Is this your psychic ability talking here?" Jose was always sharing some intuitive thought or vision with me and I loved it. He was one of my best teachers. "I'll let you know if it happens."

I thought now was a good time to bring up his partner. "I hate to bring this up but do you know what you're going to do about Rubio?"

"About him? Are you kidding? I can't do anything about him. It's me. I'm my problem."

"He's the one out all night and you're the problem? I don't get it."

"Exactly that…." The sadness in Jose's eyes tore at my heart. "He figures he can get away with this, and he does, only because I don't do anything about it. The thing is that I want to trust him. It came up in my Itá.

"What's that? Itá?" I asked, eager to learn more. It was hard enough being fluent in Spanish and English but learning the language of Yoruba was an added expectation

I'd never anticipated when attracted to the Orisha tradition. I'd grown up in New York raised by mostly English speaking parents so as much as I hated to admit it, Spanish was a second language to me.

"When a person is initiated they receive a major spiritual shell reading. The shells speak. It's a divination of everything that's occurred, happening now, and will happen... kind of like a life book. The tricky part is figuring out how it translates in the day to day. I need to watch out for things like this."

"Like what? The shells said that Rubio would be stepping out on you?"

"No, hey, what was that?" Jose picked up the clicker and turned up the volume. "Listen, it's about your job."

"No way!"

We stared at the screen. A reporter stood in front of the Emergency Room doors at Windsor. The neighborhood gentrification had done wonders for its appearance. The hospital's recently refurbished appearance was financed by private donations that had steadily trickled into the once almost impoverished hospital. The reporter's waxen face came to life as he spoke into the microphone and began recounting news about its staff.

"Hospital spokesperson, Jack Richards, is preparing to give a statement about the death of Doctor Arthur Campbell, a well-known surgeon at Windsor Medical Center, whose body was found early this morning on the hospital premises."

The televised spot was abruptly stopped as the network moved into a commercial break.

"Oh no, I don't believe it! I was there yesterday. He was there too, doing surgery... cosmetic surgeries, all day. I don't believe it. Sixth Saturday!" I was in shock.

"What are you talking about? Sixth Saturday?"

"Ssh, wait, listen." I pointed to the flat screened television. "There's Jack from Human Resources. He must hate being on T.V. like this!"

Jack Richards took his place in front of the cameras. The sounds of the reporters shouting questions at him didn't divert him from sticking to his rehearsed statement.

"We are confirming that Doctor Arthur Campbell's body was found this morning on the premises. We have no further details at this time. We would like to offer our sincere condolences to Doctor Gloria Price and to the Campbell family." Jack went a step further. "We would also like to assure our community that the hospital is at full service capacity and that we stand by our security precautions. Thank you, all."

The television camera swerved away from the hospital spokesman and swept the small crowd of people that had gathered. In the background, an ambulance backed up, its alarm beeped and policemen directed pedestrians around the scene. The segment ended and a weather commercial soon followed.

"These spots are way too short. That's Channel One for you. It'll repeat all day without any added information." I was irritated by the poor treatment of the report of Dr. Campbell's death. I wanted to know more. "I can't believe it, Doctor Campbell... dead?"

"Who's Doctor Campbell?" Jose dug into his scrambled eggs. "Is he important there?"

"We were just talking about him yesterday. I have to call Allie. I wonder what she's heard. We all worked together when he was Chief Resident. He's an Attending now and his wife is the Chief Surgical Resident."

"Not anymore, is he?"

"I guess you're right. Maybe I should contact my

boss."

"Sophia? Now?" Jose asked. "You think that's a good idea?"

I was starting to get jittery and my legs began bouncing. It was a habit that I had a hard time breaking. I was a nervous wreck. "Of course, she's the Administrator. She's got to be involved. That means I am too. This is exciting but in a weird sort of way. I knew him."

My smart phone began to vibrate and I answered it. Sophia wanted me there ASAP and I hurried to run out of the apartment.

"Gotta go, seems the hospital is a circus right now and we've got plenty to do. I hate to leave my breakfast but thanks, I love you."

"No you're not, Daisy. I love you too, but remember what we heard at the meeting this morning, 'First things first,' and that means breakfast."

I hesitated for a minute because I knew he was right. I sat back down. "I guess you're right. It may be too late for Doctor Campbell, but it's not for me."

Jose smiled and gave a half bow. "You got it."

We finished breakfast while we speculated about the death. Suddenly, the front door opened.

Rubio stood there in all his glory. A night out didn't do anything to mar the brilliance of the long dark blonde hair that was set against his creamy white skin. He wore a faded leather jacket and a pair of jeans. He seemed uncertain but definitely looked magnificent.

"Hi."

"I've really got to be on my way." I planted a kiss on Jose's cheek. He had to know that I had his back. "I'll call you later."

Brushing past Rubio, I stopped to give him a kiss too. I closed the door behind me and went back to my apartment to get ready for work. Sunday was turning into a Monday.

Chapter 3

The hospital was within walking distance of my house. The neighborhood had woken up by this time. A line of people stood in front of Dizzy's, a favorite neighborhood eatery, eager to get their Sunday brunch on. Children whizzed by on their scooters and their parents lagged behind, treasuring the lazy morning. It was amazing how the community vibe had changed within a few short hours.

As I got closer to the hospital, I saw that there were multiple media vans blocking the area. Parking was a dreaded experience in the hospital vicinity already and television coverage of the death was going to make it worse. I'd been tempted to run out of Jose's place without taking a breath and was glad that he suggested I take a minute to take care of myself first. I was relieved that I'd chosen a smart pair of casual pants with its matching jacket to cover my gauzy orange blouse. The fall days were warm enough for me to still pick from some of my summer things. I enjoyed the feel of the fabrics against my body. The possibility of me being on television was now another reason I was glad I'd gotten rid of my torn and holiest of holy jeans.

Brushing past the horde of reporters, I entered the hospital and nodded at the security guard who kept stoic watch but was friendly enough to recognize staff members. After having been there for several years I was friendly with most of the guards.

"I see that Miss Sophia had you come in on your day off." The guard grinned as I passed by. Her extravagant coiled hairdo framed her pudgy face. The dark blue uniform she'd squeezed into was severe in its cut.

I smiled and shrugged. "I could never have it as

good as you, Betty. You have a ringside seat."

"Ain't I lucky?" Betty's grin turned wry. "Ya gotta be in it, to win it."

"Ain't that the truth? Tell me about it." I gave her a small wave and tucked myself into the crowded elevator. I made sure to pull my identification card out of my bag and hung it around my neck. When I got to the office, I bumped smack into Sophia who was bustling out with a capital B.

"Good, you're finally here. What took you so long? Get your pad and pen, follow me. We're going to meet with Mister Donaldson."

"The C.E.O.?"

Mr. Donaldson always made me anxious especially when he leered at me. I started to bite at the inside of my lower lip at the thought; this was better than my awful right eye twitch. No one ever mentioned it but I felt it and could never control it. I tried to stick to my job duties but he never noticed. Ignoring his off handed compliments and observations about my "little shape" or about how nice my neckline was had become aggravating. I knew that one day I'd have to stop him in his tracks and remind him about the hospital sexual harassment policy that everyone had to follow… including the C.E.O.

"I realize that he makes you uncomfortable, Daisy, but there's been a death here."

Sophia had a way of jostling me back into focus. I ran into my office and picked up the yellow legal pad. I couldn't find my pen. I remembered looking for one yesterday at the Ambulatory Surgery clinic. Thinking about the pen got me to thinking about Dr. C. and his being found dead and the implications that could lead to. Maybe I'd find out about more of the details in my meeting with Sophia and Mr. Donaldson. That old guy was annoying but probably harmless. I grabbed a ball point from Sophia's desk and ran to follow behind her.

I caught up with her at the elevator. Sophia was wearing red, her 'stay away' color. She had the tendency to wear colors that let you know what she was thinking without saying a word. Her eyeglasses, hung by a necklace of bright red beads, rested on her more than ample bosom. She had eye glass necklaces that matched her every mood. Even the fire department would stay away from Sophia when she was in one of her bullish moods. Because of her stocky frame and her bullet-like quickness, most people tried to veer away from her when she was on one of her missions; and today was one of those days.

We rode on the elevator in silence. The few other passengers were strangers. There was no way to tell whether they were visiting ill relatives or were there for a scoop on Dr. Campbell's untimely demise. Their faces were serious, all staring forward without saying a word to one another. The elevator doors opened on the sixth floor and we rushed over to Mr. Donaldson's office.

The C.E.O. met us at the door. He'd moved past the secretary, Ms. Durand, who stood there wringing her hands. She wasn't her usual cool and crisp self. Too much was happening that was out of the ordinary; there was no way to prepare for a day like today.

"Come in, come in. You too, Daisy." Mr. Donaldson's voice shook. His black framed glasses were smeared with what had to be oatmeal. His tie was sloppy too. I'd never seen him looking like this. Mr. Suave was ready to take a nose dive.

"Pull yourself together, Ralph," Sophia instructed. "It won't do, with you looking like you've just been caught pants down on the potty. The media will have a field day with that." Sophia was clearly in charge and motioned for me to sit next to her at the round mahogany table and chair set in his large office. The window overlooked busy Seventh Avenue. I took a peek at the street before settling in next to Sophia. It had become a three ring circus and the audience was quickly growing.

I watched as Mr. Donaldson straightened his tie and ran his fingers through his short salt and pepper colored hair. He looked like Larry Tate, Darren Stevens' boss, on the old black and white Bewitched series. I swallowed a giggle and watched him pace across his office floor.

"Oh, Sophia," he moaned. "What next? We can't afford this type of publicity. Park Hill has just opened a new ambulatory surgical care unit in Sunset Park. This couldn't have happened at a worse time."

"I hope you don't mind me being direct but that's not our problem. We can't afford to go under so we'd better hang on. Death by murder and death by poor business acumen are two very different ways to die. Once you get a hold of yourself, you'll see what I mean."

The C.E.O. stopped his frantic walk and took a seat.

"Let's get down to exactly what happened. The detectives will be asking us questions at any minute and we need to be prepared. We have to look at what security measures were in place yesterday." Sophia looked at me. "Are you ready to get this down?"

I would have preferred to use my laptop or a recording device, even an iPad, but Sophia's old fashioned ways stood in the way of technology. Note taking was increasingly complicated; I created my own system. When I described it to Jose he called it an 'allegorical trajectory of symbols.' He had a much better way with words than me. The important thing was that my system, whatever I called it, worked for me. It might not for a successor but that wasn't something I worried about, too often. In other words, I put my pen to pad.

"It seems Doctor Campbell was here yesterday." Sophia poured a glass of water from the crystal pitcher that was placed on the table into a matching glass. "He completed several surgeries. Daisy, weren't you here yesterday as well?"

"Yes, it was Sixth Saturday. But I didn't actually see him. He didn't come out to the front area at all."

"I understand you worked with Alejandra Betancourt?"

"We were the pre-op admissions staff yesterday. We did the paperwork and stuff."

"Stuff." Sophia shook her head. "Can you be little more specific about this stuff?"

"Well, I did the paperwork, like the advance directives, living wills…"

"Yes, yes, but what about Ms. Betancourt? What did she do all day?"

"Allie made sure the preop labs were on the charts and in order. She made sure that the clients' vital signs were taken and charted. Kind of ran the whole pre-op area. She was supervising the new assistant…"

"Yes, yes, I know all that. Tell me, did anything out of the ordinary happen?" Sometimes she was so dismissive. Her voice seemed to have dropped an octave. "Try to focus. Did anything go on with Doctor Campbell that we need to be aware of? Or with Doctor Price, for that matter?"

My eyelid began to twitch. "Not really. The only thing was that one of his patients almost coded. But it turned out that her blood pressure had just gone down a bit. That happened toward the end of the shift. Allie told me that they were going to send her to the Recovery Room or maybe they said the Intensive Care Unit. There was a nurse there that was going to take over because they didn't want to send her home too quickly."

"Understandable." Sophia squinted her eyes. "Daisy, I need you to really think, is there anything else out of the ordinary?"

"Not really." I thought hard about yesterday's details. It seemed to be just another day at work. I could do it with my eyes closed. I shook my head. "It was a usual Sixth Saturday… people coming in for their lifts. The docs working fast. Everyone wanting to get out early."

Mr. Donaldson and Sophia shared a look. "Okay, thank you, Daisy," Sophia said. "You can wait for me back down at the office."

"Wait, can I ask a question?" I decided to ask the question that had been nibbling at the back of my brain.

"Yes?" By the turn of her mouth it was clear that Sophia wasn't happy with my request.

"I didn't get much from the television newscaster's account of what actually happened. They were pretty short on information. I was hoping you could tell me the details about his death. I'm kind of nervous. I was there all day yesterday."

Sophia peered at me over her half-moon eyeglasses. "He was found with a puncture wound in his right fifth intercostal space. The wound was made with what they believe to be a scalpel which they found on the floor next to him. The puncture went right through the lung. He either lost his balance during the attack or he was pushed and fell. The forensic team also believes that Doctor Campbell hit his head against the bench in front of his locker."

I heard Sophia speaking but the words began to echo. My brain began to throb. I couldn't believe what I was listening to. Trying to gain composure I held onto the table. I closed my eyes for a minute and when I reopened them Sophia and Mr. Donaldson were staring at me.

"Wait, he was killed? He was stabbed? But, wait,

what you're saying is that maybe he didn't die of the stab wound?"

"The autopsy report is pending but it's most likely he would have survived if it weren't for the fall. Doctor Campbell was in excellent physical condition, as you well know. He would have managed to get help. The fall and the fact it all happened post regular hours, I'm sure, were factors in his death. It must have been empty in that area for him to have died that way."

I was perplexed. "I don't get it. Did he even get out for his daily run? He always ran in Prospect Park right after surgery. The timing had to be off."

"Apparently he had to check on Mrs. Stills. She'd been sent to the Recovery Room."

I began to piece together the chain of events. "He must have gone to see her. Made sure she was all right and came back to shower. Doctor C. was so O.C.D. He said he showered before he ran to wash the O.R. experience away. I wonder if he actually did shower."

"Yes, he did."

"How do you know?"

Sophia cleared her throat. "He was dressed in a towel. He was found lying on the floor. Half..."

"Naked," I said, finishing her sentence for her. "I get the picture. What a way to die... so vulnerable. He trusted being there in the O.R. It was like his second home."

Mr. Donaldson dropped his head into his hands and cradled it.

"Is that all, Daisy?" Sophia was again dismissive. "Please wait for me at the office."

"Sure," I said. On my way back I tried to figure out why they had questioned me. That wasn't about taking minutes for the meeting. They already knew that Mrs. Stills was in the Recovery Room. They wanted to know how much information I had to help them. I hadn't given them anything new.

As I cleared away some of the clutter on my desk, I remembered the woman who came in while I waited for Allie. The woman had disappeared before I had a chance to ask her what she wanted. But then again… the woman had said she was looking for Dr. Campbell. But why?

❀

The sun glowed red and was low on the horizon that afternoon when I finally left and stood at the corner of the hospital. The mix of pink and blue clouds was heady. The evening breeze promised that true autumn would be on its way soon. Beautiful days of Indian summer always left me feeling nostalgic. It wasn't something that I could quite put my finger on but it was like listening to a minor chord. It struck something within me like a sad vibration.

While the hospital administration wanted to appear that business was going as usual, the media vans that hummed next to the police cars that were in front of the building told a different story. I decided to hike up to the quiet of Eighth Avenue, anything to avoid the mothers and the huge strollers that took up most of Seventh Avenue and the runners and cyclists on Prospect Park West. I didn't want to feel like finding out whether I still had my dodge ball skills. The afternoon had been challenging enough. Sophia and Mr. Donaldson had called me back up to his suite. I had to bite my tongue a few times to not jump in whenever either one of them started going in wide circles trying to get information from me while they speculated. Listening to all the conjecture about Dr. Campbell's canny ability to charm half the women at Windsor Medical Center was a bit nauseating.

Unfortunately, I could attest to Dr. Campbell's "charming" behaviors. It was hard for me to listen to them talk about him. I had fallen for him before I'd gotten sober. Being at my lowest point in life wasn't a good excuse but in that state it was easy to get involved with him. My first impression was that he was a gentleman. He acted so gallant when he was at the unit. His black wavy hair was highlighted with dashes of silver that made him irresistible to many women. He wore his reading glasses at work a lot and that hid his shrewd but deep violet colored eyes. They were a lot like Elizabeth Taylor's smoldering eyes when she played in Cat on a Hot Tin Roof. Dr. C. also knew how to make anyone around him laugh. He was gifted as a surgeon and a man.

Our fling sparked and fizzled fast and hard. Still, it went on long enough for me to realize that he wasn't that friendly image that he projected. In fact, he was quite the opposite. He hadn't treated me badly but watching as he so easily put the female server down when we went out to dinner was enough to make me avoid him after it was over between us. That rang too much like my days with Lou and that was something I promised myself never to go through again. I didn't want to sit at the edge of my seat waiting for him to insult me. While I didn't want him dead, I wasn't suffering that much from the loss as I knew many of the staff would be when the word of his death reached everyone.

When Sophia called it a day, I was relieved. I was sure that the next day we'd be huddled together once again. The detectives were going to speak with me in the morning. Since I hadn't actually worked with him on Saturday they'd held off. There were enough people to concentrate on that had been in the Operating and Recovery Rooms. I hadn't set eyes on him the entire day, not even once. Dr. Campbell used the back entrance to the Operating Suite. The doctors didn't have to pass the clients on their way in or out of the unit. It would be too anxiety provoking for both the client and doc. I imagined a patient introducing a prized spinster daughter to her surgeon in hopes that she would be seen as a fine catch. I stopped myself from thinking more about it. I was off and needed to chill out.

Nearing home, I saw that the entire brownstone was lit except for my apartment. That meant that everyone was probably indoors. They were missing out on the sunset. I started to climb the outside set of stairs and then changed my mind. It was a good time to visit my landlady, Marge. I loved sitting at her huge kitchen butcher block counter eating freshly baked muffins and drinking herbal teas. The woman was more like a dear friend than a dreaded landlady- as most of them had been in my previous living situations. But that probably had more to do with me not paying my rent on time or leaving the radio on at high volume when I left my apartment. I used to think that would deter would-be burglars. The days of paranoia were behind me and I hoped that my peace of mind would last forever.

Entering the old building, I stopped to say a short prayer giving thanks to whoever it was that found me that apartment and I didn't mean Jose or Rubio- although I could never thank them enough for steering me in the right direction. It had to be a guardian angel. I lived at the apartment for a little over one year and I still had to convince myself that I belonged there. I had a family, that's for sure, but I once heard that sometimes families created without blood ties could be stronger than biological ones.

I poked my head into the first floor garden apartment.

"Marge, it's me, Daisy," I called out into the

kitchen. "I've got to tell you what's going on at work. It's altogether creepy. You'd appreciate it." I placed my bag and jacket to the side of the staircase.

"Come in and close the door behind you. I think this house is getting draftier by the day," she said as she waved me in. Marge was tiny but seemed even more so when she was dwarfed by the large cast iron stove.

"I think it's colder inside than it is outside." I shivered. "You might want to ask Jose if he can find where the draft is coming from."

The house was beautiful but over a century old. Renovations would have made a world of difference but then again I probably wouldn't be living there if there had been any repairs or reconstruction done. The old world appeal would also have disappeared into sheetrock and plaster.

"I was just about to pour a cup of tea. Would you like some?" Marge turned the flame up under the steel kettle. Despite it being chilly in the room, the house was comforting- something that I and "the boys", as Marge called Jose and Rubio, always appreciated.

"I'll have some chamomile if you don't mind. No distractions for me tonight."

I sat down next to Ruffian, Marge's Seeing Eye dog, and rubbed the golden retriever's silken hair along his back. Marge was legally blind and had worked with him for about two years. It was almost impossible to tell that she was visually impaired with the ease in which she moved around the house. Ruffian snorted a bit as he settled into a nap. He was definitely off duty.

"Still not sleeping?" Marge asked. "Is something wrong or is it your usual insomnia?"

"I guess you didn't see the news today?"

"I watched T.V. but only in bits and pieces. The

baseball season is done. If there had been a Mets game on, you know I would have been glued to the set."

"They found one of the surgeons at the hospital I work at dead today," I blurted out. "Murdered! I used to work with him."

"My goodness! Tell me the details."

"I didn't know what happened from the news spot. They don't really tell much. I found out because I had to meet with my boss and the C.E.O. today. It seems the maintenance worker found him. He was finishing up his last rounds before handing the keys over to the day shift. Doctor Campbell was found lying on the floor next to his locker."

"Do they know what exactly happened to him?" Marge was gentle. "I'm so sorry about your friend."

"Thanks, Marge. I guess I am more upset than I thought I was." This was the first time since hearing about his death that my eyes began to tear. "I guess you could say that he's from a past life. But yes, he was stabbed with a scalpel. It was on the floor next to him. Whoever did it must have just dropped it." I sighed. "Apparently, they also found a big bump or something on his head, I'm not sure, but they say he also hit his head on the bench in front of his locker."

"Oh my, Daisy," Marge commiserated. "That sounds terrible."

"Imagine, getting killed by the tool of your trade. It's just awful. The staff was getting ready to start their shift. They're in by five. It seems that Doctor C. never made it home last night. They found his running clothes near him. He used to run at all hours in Prospect Park. Everyone warned him about going out there at night, in the dark. He used to brag that he could outrun any thief or crack head," I said, remembering how he used to dismiss all the warnings so easily. "Right at his job... dead." The thought hit me like a hammer.

"Terrible business, isn't it? The hospital must be swarming with police." The kettle began to whistle and Marge turned off the burner readying to pour the boiled water into the mugs.

I nodded. "I'll be questioned, for sure, tomorrow morning. I was there all day yesterday. Talk about synchronicity and not in a good way. I rarely do Sixth Saturday but I wanted to make extra bucks."

"Sixth Saturday?" Marge asked. "I've never heard that term."

"None of the surgeons want to be there on the weekends. The board is constantly thinking up new ways to make money. The administration thought up Sixth Saturdays. Every six weeks the doctors take turns in performing uncomplicated elective surgeries. Childcare, jobs, school– whatever reasons, keep a lot of people away from elective, cosmetic surgeries. Yesterday was Doctor Campbell's turn."

"What you're saying is that everyone on staff knew he'd be there. They must have a schedule posted for the entire hospital."

"It's put up at the beginning of the month, so yes, that's true," I said. "But he wasn't supposed to work since he switched with Doctor Hagar. It's a long story but he'd been on his honeymoon and made the switch. Client names aren't on that list because it's posted and the hospital makes sure to honor confidentiality, you know, HIPAA rules. The doc list is put out the day before the surgeries. So, yes, anyone of the staff would know he was scheduled to be in surgery. That leaves it wide open where staff is concerned. All the units get the list. Why, I don't know and never will understand."

Marge sipped her tea. "That is eerie, I must say. Do you really think that it was a staff member? It might have been an outsider who gained access to the area."

"Maybe." I shivered again and not because it was chilly in the room. "Feel my arms… my hair just stood straight up. Why do you think that happened?"

A blast of cool air came in through the door. I wheeled around just as Marge folded her arms against her chest.

Chapter 4

"Because you're psychic." Jose sailed into the kitchen. "There's something there that's talking to your gut."

"What are you trying to do?" I said. "I'm creeped out enough as it is without you coming in like the ghost of Christmas past."

"Jumpy, aren't you? Sorry." He laughed. "How do you put up with scaredy cat here, Marge?"

"I think he's right," Marge said. "Don't dismiss it when things like that happen. It's us getting in touch with our intuitive sides."

"Or it could be that I'm scaring myself silly, thinking about the whole thing. Allie, the nurse I worked the shift with, and I were the last of the front staff to be there yesterday. I didn't really actually see Doctor C. at all. I don't know if she did. What am I saying? Of course she did. There was a code, but it was a mistake. The patient was all right. Allie went back into the locker area at the end of the shift to change. The male and female locker rooms are right across from each other. Come to think of it, she came out with her scrubs in her hand and stuffed them in her bag. She said she had to wash them. Why didn't she throw them into the hamper like everyone else does?"

"Take a breath; you're getting a little paranoid. Do you really think your co-worker had something to do with this?" Jose was incredulous. "Get a grip."

"You're right. I guess I'm getting a little carried away. I don't really think Allie did anything. That's impossible. I'm just tired."

"How 'bout we change the subject?" Marge turned toward Jose. "How's your job search going?"

"It's not. I've had two interviews. When they see me dressed in white, they can barely get through the questions. They practically push me out of the door. I had no idea that I'd lose my job when I got initiated. It's depressing."

I could feel my temper skyrocketing. "It's incredible; I say that you have the makings for a great lawsuit. Whatever happened to equal opportunity anything? They aren't supposed to discriminate when it comes to religious beliefs. It's not fair."

"There's no way to prove that's why I was let go. My company gave me and two other employees pretty decent severance packages with our pink slips. Let's face it, there are a lot financial companies downsizing if not altogether shutting down."

"It's so hard when you don't know…" I started trying to figure it out. It was upsetting to see my best friend still unemployed. Up until he was initiated in the tradition he was a valued worker at his place of business. Then again, he was right about the financial world being a tough spot that was extremely competitive.

"That's why I've decided that this year I'm not going to take anything personally. I refuse to do that." Jose looked dejected despite his well-intentioned words.

"Wise choice, but maybe you can ask your godfather if you can wear a regular suit to your next interview," Marge advised.

"I agree." I broke in to get my next point across. "Ask Hector. He's your Padrino. A godfather is supposed to know what's going on in the real world. While dressing in white is traditional, your work isn't one where you can really walk around like that. This isn't the Caribbean."

"It was my idea. Not Hector's. He gave me the option. I've been trying to do everything by the book."

"There is no book. There have to be accommodations made for different people. How about police officers? Do you think that they wear white when they're iyawos? No way. They wear their uniforms and change into white when they get home after their shifts."

"Wow, I can see you've been doing your homework." Jose chuckled. "Now the thing I'm not sure about is whether you've been researching the religion or how to become a cop."

"Ha ha, very funny." I knew he was trying to be light about the situation but the whole thing still rankled. "I know that I'm right. You should try wearing a regular suit. You have experience. I'll bet you're hired first thing on your next job interview."

"I say we drink our tea and break into the cookies." Marge went over to the tin on the shelf under the kitchen bay window and began pulling out a freshly baked stash of oatmeal pecan cookies. "It's a great way to cap the day."

"I almost forgot to tell you this one." I stopped for a second to munch on a cookie. It was soft and tasty and still warm. "There was a woman who came looking for him. She looked like a pixie or something. I guess maybe I spend too much time reading about this stuff. I swear she couldn't have been real but she left before I had a chance to really talk to her. She was gone in a flash."

"There's something about this that rings important." Marge seemed to be searching through the veils for answers. Although she couldn't see with her eyes, she had the best intuition I'd come across. She'd been an active spiritualist when she was a younger woman.

"You'll see what I mean. This will all come clear, eventually. Why don't you take another cup of Chamomile up to bed with you? It'll do you good, help you sleep." Marge reminded me of my sleepless nights.

"Good idea, I think I'll do just that."

"I'm out of here too." Jose went over and gave Marge a hug. "Thanks for being you. You scared us with that broken hip. Don't do that again."

"Promise. Good night and don't worry so much. Everything will work out, you'll see."

"Believe me, I keep the faith but thanks for the support. I definitely depend on it."

We walked up the stairs together, passing the second floor where Marge had her bedroom and parlor with her baby grand in it. We moved her bed down to the first floor several months earlier when she fell down the stairs. Her rehab goal was to climb the flight and still have enough energy to play her beloved piano. I had no doubt that one day it would happen. Together we'd make sure it did.

We parted at the third floor and I went up the last flight to my apartment. Making it inside my door, I decided to keep it slightly open, just in case Ms. G. wanted to come up to share my bed. It was lonely in there.

※

There were no curtains or drapes to cover the silvery light that washed into the room. It was entirely illuminated by the large harvest moon. I perched on the window seat looking out onto the Sycamore lined city street. Across the way, a few of the homes had carved pumpkins displayed on the steps. I pulled my thick robe closer to my body, protecting myself against the coolness of the night. I would have preferred to be in a deep sleep nestled under my toasty warm comforter but I loved the stillness that surrounded me.

Waking up each night at three in the morning was becoming a pattern. It was the witching hour. The time of night when every spirit thought it had the right to make an appearance even when they weren't invoked. I'd found myself lying with my eyes wide open. There was no sound, just a feeling that I needed to be alert. Some nights I heard murmurings or laughter that seemed to come from the upstairs apartment except that I lived on the top floor of the building and there really wasn't anyone walking on the roof. The sound was far away yet present- eerily present.

The spirits' persistent attempts at contact were becoming almost unreasonable. Hector, Jose's godfather, had given me sage advice. If you're unavailable, let the spirit know. Set boundaries; let them communicate if and when you want. Let them know it's you who's running the show, not them. Do this especially if you're frightened. Never let them know if you're afraid. Those were the earliest of lessons he shared as he began to explain the world of spirits to me. According to Hector, I was a natural but there was still so much to learn if I expected to be a spiritualist- something I became more and more fascinated about.

"Whoever you are, you've got to give me a break. I need to sleep. You wake me up but don't say a thing. Okay, let's see if I can make you talk."

I went over to my desk and pulled out a basket filled with various tarot decks that I began collecting when I was fifteen years old. Having my own place meant that I didn't have to hide them from Lou's prying eyes and hands. Although he had no interest in them, he would touch them just to annoy me. That was as bad as my mother's attitude towards my fascination with tarot cards. She would tell me awful stories of what might happen if I were to follow in my aunt's shoes. My tía was an 'Espiritista' and most of the family was terrified of what she knew but mostly of what she might say.

I began by lighting a candle and burning some sage,

I took a minute to center myself. I closed my eyes and rummaged through the basket, willing the deck that wanted to speak to practically jump into my hands. A moment later I had it, the traditional Rider-Waite. After shuffling, I set the cards in front of me face down and let my hands do the rest of the pulling. Keeping my mind clear, I pulled one and turned it over on the table revealing the Page of Wands.

Something new was going to enter my life. Something that was fun, creative, and filled with passion. Maybe I'd be involved with a new endeavor. Being open and allowing whatever this new thing was hopefully wouldn't be too much of a challenge. My new plan was to approach life in a relaxed way- 'to wear it like a loose garment.' So far it was like a tightly buttoned oxford that was suffocating me. I didn't want to be strangled any longer.

Soft fur rubbed against my ankle.

"I thought cats were supposed to be seen and not walked into in the middle of the night." Bending down to stroke the black and white fur, I ended up cuddling the six pound ball of fluff. "Okay, sweetie, you can stay with me tonight. I'm sorry I'm such a grump. Lord knows I need some company."

Lying in bed, I thought about the last several nights of awakenings. Trying to connect with the spirits as if they were regular people seemed like a lost cause. From now on, instead of begging to the open air, I decided that I would pull a card or maybe just meditate. It was my prerogative not to sit there in misery. Ms. G. nestled in my arms and we fell fast asleep.

Chapter 5

I jumped out of bed the minute the alarm went off the next morning. No way did I want to be late on the morning that I was going to be questioned. I had a flash of the first and what I thought would be the last time I was questioned by the police. It was after Lou had catapulted down the stairs. No one had really cared at the time, only me, his mother, and aunt. The officers practically said good-bye and good riddance. They were right in a way but I still felt so guilty about it. I remembered how awful the funeral had been. I had to clear my mind. It wouldn't help going to work all muddle brained. I stood under a cold shower hoping that would do the trick. When I finally got out my skin was bright red and I hurried to get dress. I picked out the most somber outfit I could find. When I looked in the mirror I saw that somehow somber equaled stylish- New York stylish that is. My black pencil skirt and tight knit top showed off my figure. I gained some weight in the last year and I liked what I saw in the mirror.

It was way before nine when I sat at my desk. Before I knew it the phone rang. It was Ms. Durand telling me the detectives were ready to question me.

I pulled out my compact and checked to make sure I was perfect before I left the office. They last thing I needed was for them to see me without my lip gloss. My sponsor, Angela, was always reminding me that my feelings were more important than my appearance but I was nervous and looking good usually helped boost my confidence. I puckered up in the mirror and was happy with the results.

As I prepared for the interview I wondered about the types of questions they might ask me. I worked at Windsor for several years and there were so many personalities that worked there with me. I probably knew more about them than they knew about themselves. Before this tragic event, I went to the C.E.O.'s office a handful of times to bring an envelope or a file to his secretary. In the last couple of days, however, it seemed as if I practically moved in.

The elevator doors slid open and I knocked on the door leading to the Mr. Donaldson's suite. Ms. Durand, back to her usual composed self, ushered me into an inner office. The room was perfect for questioning. There was an enormous dark polished wood conference table surrounded by upholstered leather chairs. The windows took up the expanse of the south west wall revealing the view of a low rise building that housed several other medical offices. It was nothing to boast about. The first floor housed a Barnes & Noble Bookstore. Brooklyn had its zoning laws that were maddening to community prospectors but kept the brownstone neighborhood residents quite contented.

"Miss Muñiz?" There were two detectives sitting at the table. Both stood up when I walked into the room. "I'm Detective Rodriguez and this is my partner, Detective Munroe."

Detective Rodriguez looked like he'd taken his Detective 101 course very seriously. He was tall, dark, and the outline of his muscles could be seen through the fabric of his custom made suit. All that was missing was a brimmed fedora. He had the makings of a classic Humphrey Bogart in The Big Sweep. Very forties. Very sleek. He reached out to shake my hand. His fingernails were manicured. I couldn't help but notice he wasn't wearing a wedding band. I quickly imagined us in a scenario that made me skip a breath. I cleared my throat in order to bring myself back to the world of reality.

Taking Detective Munroe's hand next, I saw that

her manicured nails were polished a deep burgundy. I met her unyielding gaze and it softened as she gave me a quick smile. She wore a complementing shade of lipstick.

"Detective Munroe," the woman said. She stood back and pushed her long silky blond hair away from her face. She looked as though she also spent hours chiseling away at her body at the gym. As I noticed her form fitting suit, I was relieved that I chose the outfit I did that morning. We made a fashionable and sophisticated New York City trio.

"We have some questions we'd like to ask you. Please have a seat." Rodriguez pulled one of the chairs away from the table. His voice was a deep baritone. I liked what I heard but then I remembered that I was being questioned about the death of a man I'd been involved with. This was the second time in a little over a year and I needed to change that.

"So, tell us about Saturday, Miss Muñiz," Detective Rodriguez questioned me. "We understand you were here at the hospital."

He smiled at me and I couldn't help but admire his even white teeth. Great against his trigueño, caramel colored skin. One of my tribe, I could see, and a very attractive member at that.

"Yes, I was here on Saturday."

"Isn't that odd? You're the administrator's secretary, aren't you?"

"Yes, I worked as a clerk for a few years before I was promoted as her assistant. This is a new position for me."

Detective Munroe raised her eyebrows but remained silent. There didn't seem anything puzzling in how I described my job promotion as far as I could tell. Maybe I was making a bigger deal of it than I should. These questions were a formality. I was there on Saturday. It didn't mean that they thought I was the murderer.

"So you've been around Windsor Medical Center for a while?"

"Yes." It wasn't a court room but I watched enough television to know not to give away too much information.

"So, you knew Doctor Campbell?"

"Yes." My face flushed again and turned warm. I cursed myself under my breath.

"Excuse me, I couldn't quite catch that." The detective used a hand held electronic device to record the information he obtained from me. Gone were the days of little black note books.

"Yes, I knew him. We worked here together for a while."

"Of course." Detective Munroe smiled again and flashed a glimpse of her lovely porcelain overbite. "Go ahead, Rod."

I realized that I was sitting forward in my chair. I sat back, determined not to show how nervous I was actually feeling. 'Rod.' that had to be short for Rodriguez... it couldn't be his first name. 'Focus, Daisy, focus', I called myself back.

Detective Rodriguez pursued the topic. "I'm not sure you told us why you were working at the surgical clinic on a Saturday morning?"

"They do mini plastic surgery on Saturdays once every six weeks. You know, for people who can't make it on the usual Fridays. It's kind of like a spa- or at least that's how people like to describe it..."

"Surgical spa?" Rodriguez's eye brow cocked.

"It's new. People like it. They get their necks tightened and other stuff too. Most times these procedures are done on Fridays..."

Munroe interrupted. "Tell us why you were there on Saturday." I couldn't help but notice that her creamy complexion was flawless. No benzoyl peroxide in this woman's medicine cabinet.

"Sometimes I work on Sixth Saturday- that's what we call it- to make extra money."

Detective Rodriguez nodded across from me. "What time were you here that Saturday?"

"We have to arrive at five a.m. to start setting things up. I was here with the admitting nurse, Allie Betancourt. The first clients get in about six. All the pre-op labs have been done and all we need to do is to check the patient in. The surgeries begin at seven. I've been doing it for a little less than a year."

When I'd gotten sober I realized that I wouldn't be able to pay off my credit cards for about twenty years if I depended solely on my regular paycheck. Allie had asked me in passing whether I knew anyone who could help out and I jumped at the opportunity. No longer waking up hung over made it for an easy morning. All I had to do was walk up to the hospital and be back home by three in the afternoon.

"Did you see Doctor Campbell that morning?"

"No, I didn't."

"Wasn't that strange... not seeing him when you worked on the same unit?" Detective Munroe was sharp.

"Not really. There are other entrances to the surgical suite. He usually went to peek in on any of his patients that may have had more extensive surgeries on the Friday before. He usually ran down the stairs from the fifth floor, the unit is on two- he was a healthy sort of guy."

"Healthy?" Detective Munroe walked over to the picture window and gazed out at the line of people at the shishkabob stand. "What do you mean healthy?"

"He was a marathon runner. The doctors also have a gym on site. It's attached to their locker room."

"Did he ever work out before surgery in the morning, as far as you know?"

"I don't know. We aren't allowed in the gym, only the doctors are," I said. "Anything is possible though. Doctor Campbell had an incredible energy. Like the Eveready bunny- if you know what I mean."

Detective Munroe gave me a long side glance. "Did he ever talk to you about any problems?"

"No, he didn't. We weren't really close."

I thought about the time that he spent the night at my place. At about four in the morning I turned around to snuggle but he was already gone. Truthfully, that incident stung until he told me that it wasn't about me but that he routinely got up at three a.m. to run a couple of loops in Prospect Park. I was shocked. What kind of person did that? I questioned his behavior. He shrugged it off saying he'd been doing it all of his adult life.

"He was stabbed in the back, wasn't he?" I blurted out.

The detectives looked at each other and then faced me. "What makes you say that?" Rod questioned for the two.

"My boss told me, but I can't figure out how anyone would get close to him with a scalpel. He's a fast runner." I quickly corrected myself. "He was a fast runner. No one would be able to catch up to him. He didn't know that anyone was in the room with him, did he?"

Munroe stood there like a glacier and didn't look like she was about to melt anytime soon. "There is certain information that we're unable to share at this time, Miss Muñiz. We're still investigating the murder. At this moment we're trying to rule out people."

"Detective, I'm not the murderer; you're wasting your time on me. I went to work like I always do. But I should tell you before someone else does that Doctor Campbell and I had a short fling, but that was over months ago. If you do your homework, you'll see that I'm not the only one. You might want to be on the lookout for someone who came looking for him that afternoon." I stopped short but it was too late.

"Who are you talking about?" Rodriguez's jaw was set like granite.

"Nothing, really, there was a woman who came looking for him while Allie and I were getting ready to close up shop. She was only there for a second. I spilled some water and by the time I got paper towel to clean it up she was gone."

"Did she give you a name?"

"No."

"What did she look like?"

"A pixie…"

This time Munroe squeezed her left eye shut as though she was struck by a migraine. "Can you be a little more descriptive? Do you mean she wore a dress of lights and gossamer wings?"

That type of sarcasm was the catalyst that turned my blood cold. "No, Detective, of course not, the woman had short brown hair and blue eyes. She was about 4'11".

"Any other distinguishing features?" Munroe's voice softened.

"No… yes, her voice. It was throaty. Hoarse, like she was recovering from a cold. Her coat was a velvety brown."

"Anything else that you remember?"

"No, that's about it," I said.

Rodriguez gave an almost imperceptible nod.

"Okay, that's all we'll ask for today. We might have more questions for you at a later time. You weren't planning a vacation were you?"

"Are you telling me that I shouldn't leave the country?"

"No, ma'am, but we may need to contact you again."

"I take it then that we're done here." I strode over to the door. "I have some work to do."

Chapter 6

Getting back to work was a lost cause. I was pretty upset and felt like they hadn't taken me seriously. The easiest way to lose me was to be sarcastic. It seemed as though the rest of the morning would never end and I decided to take a break. I walked out into the street in front of Windsor and pulled my phone out of my jacket pocket and touched "favorites" on the screen. Tears started streaming out of my eyes. When that happened I knew that I was stressed out, sometimes tears were my only clue.

The phone rang and immediately went to voice mail. I decided to leave a message. "Hi Letty, it's me, Daisy. Give me a call when you have time."

That felt all too familiar. When I was first sober, Letty told me that she was used to me calling her almost every day of the week and those calls didn't include the middle of the night emergency ones. Too dramatic, she said. Now I made it a point not to make annoying calls. Although to me they all seemed urgent at the time. Everything seemed to have been a matter between life and death. She practically hung up on me the night I couldn't decide whether I wanted a grilled cheese sandwich with tomato or a grilled cheese with tomato soup. Not being able to make simple decisions like those sent me over the edge. I broke down every time I couldn't make my mind up over anything and poor Letty listened to me unravel.

I walked over to the small restaurant to buy a corn muffin. I thought that if they lathered it in butter and jelly I might live after all. As I walked in the smell of diner food invaded the air, I looked at the bakery display to see if they had freshly baked muffins. Before I could order I heard my name called out from behind me.

"Daisy?" I turned around to see Rubio sitting at the counter behind a bowl of chicken noodle soup. No wonder he never gained an ounce.

"Hey, what are you doing here?" I asked.

"I needed some time to think."

"I guess this is what happens when you live in the same neighborhood you work in; you get to see who's doing what during the day."

"I'm on my way to the gallery."

"Since when are you a luncheonette type of guy?" I was puzzled. "Isn't Jose at home?"

"We needed a little time… away from each other, I mean." Rubio took a sip of his coffee.

"Everything okay?"

"You know how it is sometimes. Everybody needs a chance to breathe."

"I guess you're right. It's been so long that I've been in a relationship that I almost forgot. But, I do know how tough it can be. If you ever want to talk, let me know." I hailed the counterperson over. "Can I get a bowl of chicken noodle soup with that corn muffin to go? And a prune Danish and a coffee, skim milk, and Sweet and Low." I decided to treat Sophia to one of her favorite snacks.

I looked back at Rubio and saw the sad look in his eyes. Jose, Rubio, and I had been friends since high school but Jose and I had a deep friendship. He reached out to me when things seemed their darkest. His keen mind helped me to make sense of things.

"I think Jose could use some support, why don't you speak with him? You know, be a friend."

It was as though Rubio heard my thoughts. That was the problem with hanging around a group of spiritualists- there was a lot more synchronicity than with the usual folks I came across at work.

I felt my cheeks get hot. The mirror behind the counter reflected that they looked like ripe tomatoes. I wished I could get a hold of the habit and stop it once and for all. "Sure, I can do that but remember we're friends too." I reached over and slightly squeezed his shoulder. "Anyway, I've got to be on my way."

I paid at the counter and pocketed the change before getting out of there, it was important for me to get to the office. Sophia was suspicious enough as it was. On the way back I felt the vibration of my phone at my hip. Letty was returning my phone call.

"Hi," I said. I stood at the busy intersection but could hear music in the background.

"Hey, glad you called. I'm at lunch and then I'm planning to exchange a top I bought. What's going on? You okay?"

"There's a lot going on at work. I'm not really sure who I can talk to about it."

"Well, you can always talk to me," Letty said. "Why don't you come over for dinner later in the week? Mike will probably be home late. He's been so busy at work."

One of Letty's best assets was her spontaneity. I, on the other hand, loathed doing anything spur of the moment. These opportunities were something I had to learn to embrace; it was all part of wearing that loose garment.

"Okay, it sounds great. Just let me know what day and I'll be there. Oh, and the time too. Okay?"

"I can't believe this! I'm so happy you said yes. Something good must be going on. I remember when I had to give you a month's notice for anything. I'll text you as soon as I figure out when. Talk to you soon!"

I turned off my phone and ducked behind a

newscaster that was updating New York City on the murder of Dr. Campbell. I didn't want to be seen on television.

⁂

  The day was trying and I was glad to finally be back at home. This time after climbing under the covers, I remembered to say my prayers, and did so with my eyes on the almost full white moon. I was soon fast asleep.

  A mewing sound came from behind the door startling me and I sat upright. Attempting to gather my thoughts, I realized I'd been pulled out of a vivid dream. After collecting Ms. G. from the hallway I rummaged through a pile of books for my leather bound dream journal. The lines across the front and back covers revealed the heavy use I gave it. I picked up a pen and began to write whatever scattered bits and pieces that I could remember of my dream. Because I was still groggy it took me a few minutes to pull my thoughts together, but once I did, everything seemed to get clearer. The sequence played itself once again for me. It was one of those snippet type dreams I often had. They were pretty short but they were usually meaningful.

  The image of a man dressed in scrubs played across my mind like motion picture stills from the early 1900's. He was arguing with a smaller feminine figure. I couldn't tell if she was a nurse or a doctor because they wore the same colored scrubs but she was considerably shorter than the male. She seemed pretty curvy. Neither one's face was visible because of the surgical masks they wore. I couldn't see the details of it all. The two tussled for a moment and then the male stood alone. Somehow the woman disappeared from what looked like a picture frame and the man's figure loomed close in my mind's eye. A close up of the man's face revealed Dr. C.'s piercing violet eyes.

I dropped my pen. Maybe Sophia was right after all. The murderer could very well be a woman. It was very possible that it was one of the nurses. I desperately hoped it wasn't Allie.

Allie and I met up early the next morning and we sat next to each other on a bench in the hospital atrium. Our voices were muffled by the tree shrubs and other greenery that took up the expanse of the space. Visitors sat relaxing under the glass ceiling that subtly let in the sunlight. Most of them needed rest from the stress involved with their relatives' and friends' illnesses.

"Did you know that there's a memorial being planned for Doctor Campbell in a couple of days?" I kept my voice low. I wasn't sure if I wanted to tell her about my dream.

"I have to tell you something." Allie moved closer to me. She looked around and lowered the volume of her voice. "I spoke with Miss Taylor. You know who I mean, the nursing supervisor. She had a lot to say."

"What are you talking about? You're giving me the willies." I shivered. "When you do that with your voice it makes me nervous."

"Don't be silly," Allie said. "I just don't want anyone to hear what I'm going to say."

There were a few staff members around but they were all outside of ear shot. Just as Allie was about to speak the atrium door swung open. It was a joke believing that we had any privacy here. The place was built on illusion.

"What did she say?" I urged her to go on.

"She said that he came on to her, really strongly. Miss Taylor is not one to get too familiar with any of the doctors. She admitted that she reported him for sexual harassment."

"He came on to her?"

The supervisor was so disapproving that summer evening she'd seen Dr. C. and me in the elevator acting like teenagers. It was obvious that we had more than a few drinks. I couldn't stop laughing and he couldn't stop making me laugh. There was no official reason for us to be there that late, but he needed to look at a file on a particularly nasty case of facial moles that he planned to dissect the next day. He suggested we go pick it up before we headed over to my place for a nightcap.

I shook my head. "What was wrong with that man? She isn't the type that you play around with. She's a supervisor."

"He was a pig!" Allie was vehement. "She said that he fondled her..."

"No." I put my hand out to stop her. "Stop. That, I don't believe."

"What do you mean? Why wouldn't you?" Allie seemed confused. "You would trust Doctor Campbell over Miss Taylor?"

"Well, no, but something isn't right about that at all, Allie, think about it. Doctor Campbell could get any woman he wanted. Why would he try to get involved with someone like Miss Taylor? That kind of behavior just wasn't up his alley."

"That's what you say... I think he was capable of that. I think that it would be unexpected and that would make it all the more possible."

"I don't know."

"Why else do you think he's dead?" Allie persisted. "I bet that he was a lot worse than we thought."

"He may have been out there around women but he

wasn't a bad man, if that's what you're getting at," I said. "Do you think it was Miss Taylor?"

"Miss Taylor? The murderer?" Allie was incredulous. "Of course not! No way!"

"Whatever the truth is, I need to get back to my office before Sophia starts to wonder where I am."

"Are you leaving early today?" Allie stood up.

"No, I'm leaving at the usual time. Why, are you?"

"I heard that only the skeleton staff is required to stay after the day shift," Allie explained. "I'm tying up loose ends on the unit and then I'm going home. You couldn't get me to stay longer if you tried. I'm nervous about the whole thing."

"Nervous?" I was perplexed. "Why are you so nervous?"

"Oh, Daisy, come on." Allie sounded exasperated. "The murderer, hello, did you forget? The murderer is still on the loose."

"Yeah, yeah, I know," I said. "Somehow I thought the murderer was out for Dr. Campbell. I don't believe in that old 'wrong place wrong time' thing. Somehow I think it was just the opposite."

"Opposite? What do you mean?"

"Well, honestly, to me, I think that the murderer knew exactly what he was doing, to who and why. We just haven't figured it out yet, that's all."

"He? You mean you don't think it was a woman?"

"It might be. One in particular." The dream sequence came back to me. I opened the door and we moved into the larger corridor.

"Spit it out will you? I have to get back."

"Me too." I glanced over my shoulder again. "Do you think it's possible that it was Doctor Price?"

"Are you kidding? Those two just got married. She

thought the world of him. I don't think she'd risk losing it all."

"It could have been a crime of passion. Maybe she found out that he was a skirt chaser…"

"I think she knew that all along. Everyone did, but there was still his charm. No... I think she knew what he was about and the fixings were worth that turkey."

"Wow, Allie, sometimes you're pretty harsh. I don't know you like this."

"Like I said, I have to get back."

We headed toward the elevator. "We'll talk later, okay? I think I'll take the stairs."

"Sure."

As I walked the length of the corridor, I took in the various artworks that lined the walls. A lot of money had been put into the renovation of Windsor Medical Center. The institution was doing its best to keep a high standard of client care in both the clinical and physical aspects. People couldn't be changed though. Dr. Campbell had been at the top of his game. He had the ability to draw people from far and wide because of his excellent surgical skills. It was rare that any of his clients developed infections or swelling. He was well known across the country. His extra-curricular activities were part of his phenomena.

"Excuse me!" A staff member from Central Supply swerved the cart away from me. "Heads up, okay?"

"Sorry, you're right." I was immersed in my thoughts and wasn't paying attention to where I was walking. I was close to the operating suite and saw Dr. Price coming out of the back door to the maze of rooms that made up the suite. I'd almost forgotten about that door because no one really used it other than the surgeons who wanted to keep out of sight of the relatives and patients. Avoidant yes, but it was the only way to get work done.

Dr. Price was in a daze and looked as though she was walking between worlds. What did they call that? Dissociated? That's what Ms. Lugo from the psychiatry unit would call her. Of course she would be walking around like that. Her new husband was dead. Dr. Price was lovely. Her complexion was very pale and striking against her shiny black tresses. Her dark eyes were large and set off her ruby lips and cheeks. No wonder he married her. Dr. Price's beauty was unique in a vampirish sort of way. She was voluptuous but not as short as the woman in my dream. Could it be her? I wondered.

I watched as she took her smart phone out of her pocket and began to text. She quickly put it back and made her way in the opposite direction. There was so much that couldn't be answered. Not today, maybe never. I needed a break from my thoughts. Maybe a vacation, but that was unlikely. Dinner with my best friend would be the next best thing. Thank goodness for old friends who loved you no matter what you did or what you were going through.

Chapter 7

A bouquet of irises would be a great gift for Letty and Mike. When I picked them up from the bucket in front of the grocery store they dripped on my jacket but I didn't mind. I used to bring magnums of wine when I visited- gulping most of it while everyone else sipped from a glass or two throughout the night. There were spills on my clothes, chairs, ivory tablecloths, and area rugs. It was a miracle I was ever invited back anywhere. Being friends with Letty since high school really did have its perks. She never judged me, despite whatever happened. I grabbed a boxed apple pie off one of the shelves. Flowers and dessert would be perfect.

Their brick house was in Sunset Park. It was a family neighborhood. The fact that Mike was a police officer made the area and house feel even safer to me. Still, I was a bit anxious. I looked down at my outfit checking to see that I looked good. When I passed my reflection in the store window, it was obvious that my emotions were getting the best of me. It was my insides, not the outsides that were a bit unsettled. Rightly or wrongly so, my feelings were just my feelings, they weren't facts and I needed to keep myself in check.

Waiting at the bus stop wasn't so hard. There were lots of folks commuting from work. It would be later that evening on my way home, when the streets were quiet, that I'd be more nervous. There was always some clod who thought that I wanted to talk to them when in fact I didn't. As the bus approached the block I was pretty surprised to see it was on schedule. I climbed on, paid the fare, and sat down. The plastic around the flowers crinkled as I tried not to squish them.

I started thinking about Letty and Mike who had reunited after a brief separation. His dangerous work was too stressful for Letty who was supposed to be his support person. Mike didn't like to share the details about work because he thought she'd have more of an excuse to be stressed. They went to couples' counseling and found out their major problem was their poor communication. If only that had been the main problem between Lou and me, ours were a lot worse than that. Shortly after their reunion, Letty got pregnant with Natalia. Their son Jorgito, my godson, loved Nati. She was a cutie. As I thought about them I was beginning to feel less anxious.

The bus ride was short. I got to their block in about fifteen minutes. The three story brick building looked the same as it had when I started going there with the gang. I climbed up the outside steps and rang the bell at the second floor entrance. I preferred meeting on the outside where we could gab and not worry about little kids listening to everything but Letty was way too busy and through the years I was learning it wasn't all about me.

Jorgito spotted me through the glass and opened the door. He looked so excited and happy as he slid back and forth on the parquet floor in his white socks.

"Hi, guy!" I bent over to kiss his cool little cheek.

"Hi, Titi." I was auntie by default because of my relationship with Letty. I smiled as he continued to dance his little dance but eyed my bags. "Mommy said you were coming tonight."

I hugged him. "What are you looking for?" I laughed. "I spoil you, you know, but here." I thrust a small paper bag into his hands.

"Thanks, Titi." He opened the bag and shut it quickly. "I'm not giving any of this to the baby."

"Good idea."

"What's that?" Letty walked into the hallway from the kitchen. She reached into the bag and pulled out his favorite chocolate covered caramel candies. "Nice. You're lucky, kid, but these are for after dinner. Come on in, Daisy, you can help me out in the kitchen."

The room had been renovated several years earlier. What had been a tiny kitchen separate to a large formal dining room was now a huge open space where the large center counter had become the focal point for food prep, eating, and homework.

"Please pick up your books. We're going to be eating soon." Letty was a drill sergeant around the boy.

Without a scowl, Jorgito gathered his belongings, stuffing most of them into his backpack, and went upstairs to his room.

"I call him my little Elleguá." Letty smiled. "I know that he's only eight but he's such a little trickster. He's always been that way. He's the one that brought me and Mike back together. Sad to say, but it's true."

"Maybe that's what I need, a little Elleguá magic in my life."

"You never know." Letty cut the thick loaf of bread into several slices.

"Can I ask you something?"

"I know what you're gonna ask, why haven't I gotten initiated yet? Am I right?"

"Yes, exactly that! I've watched Hector get more and more into the religion. When I met you I think he was already initiated, wasn't he?"

"Yeah, but remember that he's older than me by about ten years. We don't have the same father. His father was a priest of Changó."

"Did I know that?" I tried to think back to when we were young girls, meeting in our freshmen year of high school. "I don't think that I remembered that at all."

"My mom remarried a few years after her divorce. That's when she had me. By that time, she'd stopped going to tambores." Letty spoke about the Sunday afternoon drummings where people connected with the Orishas. "She was never initiated but went because of Hector's father. He grew up differently than me because he was close to his Dad. He was with him on most weekends and that's usually when these ceremonies take place."

"So, you knew about it but didn't practice?"

"It was sort of like background music. I guess that's the best way to explain it." Letty looked thoughtful. "Don't get me wrong. I am interested. I have my elekes but I'd really have to think about getting crowned. That wouldn't be dipping a toe into the river; it would more be like crashing over the rocks."

"That sounds scary. Why would anyone get crowned if that's how it is?"

"It isn't really; I guess… I don't know, since I haven't actually done it. But I do know that you have to be sure that it's what you really want to do. Not easy to turn back, if you change your mind, if you can at all." Letty took several crystal glasses off the cabinet shelves. "Daisy, are you interested? I mean for you."

"Not initiated but maybe collares. It seems like it would help for a fresh new start. I've been watching Jose and he's so, well, fervent."

"Have you mentioned it to him?"

"No, he's been having a hard time with the job situation and Rubio."

"Rubio?" Letty sighed. "What's wrong with us? I know there's love there. Just like with me and Mike. What the heck is going on in the romance department?"

"Don't you think it's normal for people who have

been together for a long time to have trouble in their relationship?"

"I don't know if it's normal but it's hard when it happens. In my case, it's probably because I'm always exhausted. I wish that…"

I took a better look at Letty. She was beautiful but she did look tired. Little worry lines were starting to gather at her brows. Letty always had long hair and it was pulled into a braid that reached her lower back. She was a little on the thin side but strong. Letty never had to watch a meal in her life. I envied that at some points but right now, I didn't. She had a lot more on her plate to deal with than I did. Murder and all.

The front door opened and Letty stopped short. Jorgito practically flew down the stairs to meet his father.

"Papi!"

I watched him jump into his dad's arms. There was so much love between the two, it was powerful.

After putting the boy down, Mike came to the kitchen doorway. "I thought I wouldn't call and surprise you tonight. We got a break."

"Nice! Early is always good." Letty went over to him and they kissed while Jorgito danced up and down in front of them.

"Hey, Daisy." Mike stood aside and called out to the hallway. "Come on in. Don't be shy. I'd like to introduce you to a new colleague of mine. This is my wife, Letty. Letty, this is David Rodriguez."

I immediately felt queasy and my knees began to wobble. Detective Rodriguez… Rod.

I thought, why is this happening to me? The room quickly spun but I did my best to recover while Letty shook hands with him.

"And this is a close friend of ours, Daisy Muñiz."

"We've met." The detective extended his hand to me. "Nice to meet you again."

I took his hand briefly. "Hi."

"Don't tell me, you two know each other?" Mike seemed perplexed.

"The hospital case I'm working on."

"Of course," Mike said. "What was I thinking? Something smells good in here."

"It's just about ready. Why don't you guys have a drink in the living room? We'll get everything ready." Letty steered me into the dining room that adjoined the parlor. She pulled the tablecloth and napkins from the sideboard. "He questioned you?" she mouthed. "Why didn't you tell me about that?"

"It was better talking about other stuff. I've kind of had it with the job right now," I whispered. "He was all right. His partner is intense." I made a face. "Uptight."

"Sorry about this. Mixing business with pleasure isn't always the best, is it?"

"Don't worry about it. No problem." I peeked into the living room. The men were on the couch talking in low tones. "I think."

We set the table and sat down to eat. Both Mike and Detective Rodriguez drank the red wine that was a perfect complement to the roast. I sat there quietly thanking the heavens that I didn't feel like drinking and that the cravings had disappeared.

"I hope you're not uncomfortable with my being here, Miss Muñiz. I'm new to Brooklyn and Mike has been nice enough to make me feel a part of..." Rod began. This time he wasn't wearing his suit and had on a knit shirt that showed every ripple in his muscular chest. "I'm surprised to see you here; when Mike invited me for dinner I never suspected that you'd be here."

"Believe me, Detective, I feel the same way." I put my fork down. My nerves were on edge and I took a deep breath to relax. "But it's all okay with me. You won't get in trouble at work will you?"

"No," he said. "We just shouldn't talk about the case. By the way you can call me David or Rod, like everyone else." He took a sip of the wine and cleared his throat. "Except at the hospital... you understand."

"I'm fine with that and please call me Daisy."

Rod nodded and sipped a little more of his wine. He put his glass down. "That's it for me. I have to drive home."

"Are you far?" Letty looked up from tending to Natalia who sat in the swing set that was next to the dining table.

"Billyburg."

I couldn't help but burst out laughing.

"Hey, did I say something wrong?" Rod asked. "I just moved out here a few months ago from Chicago."

"Not really," I confided. "It's just that New York transplants tend to give nicknames when they move into the neighborhoods. We actually call it Williamsburg. At least it used to be- before it got hip. So, tell me, how is it that you're here from Chicago and already a detective on the force here?"

Rod cleared his throat again. "It's a long story… too long for tonight."

After a brief awkward silence, Mike poured himself another glass of Cabernet. "We're glad to have you here. Maybe I should have invited Munroe."

Letty piped in. "Who's Munroe?"

"My partner, her name is Munroe."

"Well, I guess I can thank you for leaving your bull dog, I mean, Detective Munroe, home," I said as I dove to pick Natalia's pacifier up from where it had rolled.

"She may seem vicious but I trust her."

My hand flew to my mouth. I didn't mean for him to hear me. 'Restraint in pen and tongue' I reminded myself. When was I going to learn that? "I'm sorry. I don't know what's gotten into me."

"She's a little icy but she's got great control and excellent skills. It's hectic out there. I'm glad to have a good partner."

"You're not kidding." Mike nodded. "I haven't been out there that long- in terms of being detective- down in Brooklyn. When I was transferred from Harlem I thought I'd have to worry about the size of my gut but, boy, was I wrong."

I pretended to be busy with the baby. Letty started to clear off the table. The issue of the transfer was a tricky subject. Letty seemed to have picked up a nervous energy. She hated the fact that at any point in the day Mike could meet up with criminals he arrested and that the families of the perpetrators might actually live in the neighborhood. It was scary. She kept quiet but looked at me. I smiled at her. There were some things that a friend really couldn't help with and just had to be ready in case something awful happened.

Rod smiled. "I know it's a little late to say this but I think you have a beautiful home. I hope to get a tour of it one day."

"Now's a good time," Letty said. "I'll put some coffee on in a few minutes. Daisy bought us a nice apple pie."

We trooped through the apartment as Mike proudly showed the different areas that had been renovated under his supervision. The actual work had been completed by contractors because of his packed work schedule. They were able to keep some of the charm of the turn of the century home while updating it with the latest appliances. We returned to the dining room after Rod showed enough exuberance to satisfy Jorgito who took the opportunity to show him his room. Mario, Spiderman, and Batman posters papered the walls.

"My mother bought this house in 1968," Mike explained. "Thank goodness she didn't sell. There were a lot of real estate offers. But my parents weren't about to give in. They lived in a small apartment when they first got here from Puerto Rico. They worked very hard but it was definitely worth it and we appreciate it."

We chitchatted about everything we could think of that didn't include the murder. Even if we could it wouldn't be right with Jorgito right there. It was a home rule that remained unbroken; no one was allowed to discuss the dark side of the police profession in front of the children. Letty and Mike were pretty good at not breaking it.

The evening wore on and I finally stood up to leave.

"Do you need a lift home?" Rod helped me on with my jacket. "How far are you?"

"Not far. I'm in the Slope." I buttoned up. "Lincoln Place... I wouldn't want to take you out of your way."

"I'm fine with driving you home. Let's go."

After we said our goodbyes, Rod led me to his car.

I took one look at it and rolled my eyes. "Are you kidding? A dark sedan? This has to be your work car."

"No, it's mine," he said. "I like low key."

"Somehow I had you figured for a large silvery thing. You know, like an SUV or something." I sounded as though I was flirting and my plan had been to stay away from exactly that.

We sat there for a minute before Rod put the key into the ignition. "I hope this isn't awkward for you."

"Me?" I asked. "You mean more awkward than being a suspect? No."

"I know my partner can be a little, how can I put this..." Rod reached for the proper wording that would describe Munroe. "Pushy?"

"Forget it. I don't expect you to excuse her or your work. I'm a suspect."

"Well, we haven't ruled anyone out, yet," he said. "But no, you're not really a suspect. You just happened to be at work that day. Isn't that what you said?"

"I sense I'm being questioned again."

"No, sorry," he said. "I've been told that I can't lose the detective way of talking, by my priest."

We both laughed.

"I'm kidding. I'm intense. That's why I'm no longer in Chicago. Not stuff I can go into right now but I was told I needed to get away. Far away. Take time to cool off, and look, here I am, right in the fire. Dealing with a murder on one of the first days I'm here."

"So you haven't been working with your partner that long have you?"

"No, we just started," Rod admitted. "I've been a detective for about five years."

"Less stressful than walking a beat, I guess?" I ventured.

"Well, it's walking a beat in a different way," Rod said. "There's always stress involved. So, I want you to tell me, off the record..."

"Off the record? Who talks like that? Is there such a thing?"

"Maybe not, but you know what I'm talking about," he said. "The woman that came over to you at the end of your shift... tell me about that."

"You really are trying to mix business with

pleasure!" I was surprised he was going down this road. "But then again, I don't know if I'm really having that much fun."

Rod pulled out of the parking space. He drove slowly. Stopped at the red light, he tried again. "It's important."

"It's exactly as I told you. A woman came to me at the end of the shift. She asked for Doctor Campbell and disappeared as quickly as she appeared. Poof! She was gone. I wasn't there when she left."

"What do you mean? You weren't there?" He hit his head lightly on the steering wheel. "So you never really did see her leave?"

"Dramatic aren't you?" I pointed to the now green light. "I spilled water on my pants and the reception desk. I went to get something to mop up the water and when I came back she was gone. That's the extent of it."

"Where are you, Lincoln and what?" Rod's eyes canvassed Eighth Avenue.

"Is this how you drive all the time? Sixth." I decided to go a little further on the pixie topic. "You know when I told you she looked like a pixie, I meant that. I know your partner thinks it's ridiculous but she did. She was tiny and had these bright blue eyes and a short brown hair cut. Pixyish."

"No, I get it," he said. "That's a description." He drove down Lincoln Place. "Between Sixth and Seventh or Sixth and Fifth?"

"Seventh."

He looked at the tree lined blocks and then at me. Rod's face was an open question mark.

"Lucky rental, that's all. No magic." Sometimes I got tired of explaining how I lived on a very exclusive block. I pointed to the house. "Right there... can I tell you something else?"

"Sure." He double-parked and put his hazards on. "Anything…"

"I had a dream. Not about her. Sometimes I get a kind of feeling or dream."

"A dream? You're gonna tell me about a dream?" He chuckled. "This will definitely be off the record."

"The tone, Detective, the tone."

"Sorry, it's just that… a dream? Where am I supposed to take that info?" Rodriguez sighed. "But go ahead…"

"Don't throw away what I'm about to tell you." I looked him square in the eye. "Look, we just met and I'm taking a chance here; I don't want you to think that I'm a lulu. I see things. Well, not really see things but I do get intuitions, dreams. Stuff like that. Just so you know, I'm not crazy."

Rod leaned on the driver's door. "So what I'm hearing is that I should take what you say seriously." He met my gaze. "Hey, I probably grew up like you. My family believes in that sort of thing." He shook his head.

"You probably didn't grow up like me, because my parents are nuts. I don't mean really mental but they're still whack. But they're my parents."

"My mother had misas when I was growing up," he admitted." Is that what you're talking about?"

"Yes, I can't believe it!" This was so exciting. "For once, I can say what I need to say. What about you…?"

"No, I stayed away from them as soon as I could. Thanks to Saturday afternoon baseball I had an excuse to leave the house. I think she mostly had them in order to find out information on my father. You know, she'd ask questions about what he was doing behind her back. She wanted to know whether he was seeing other women." He

72

was clearly uncomfortable talking about this.

"That doesn't sound good."

"Well, there was always some spirit or another who would come down and upset my mother for a few weeks," he said and half smiled. "I guess, crazy is a good way to describe it. It was, like I said, I stayed away most of the time."

"Okay, I'm just about done. It's been a long day." I unclicked my seat belt.

Rod held onto my arm. "Wait, the dream. You didn't tell me about the dream."

"Right, the dream... I dreamt that Doctor C. was arguing with a woman. It was probably a female nurse or a doctor. At the lockers. I can't say more. It was just a snippet."

"That's it?"

"That's it. Sorry."

"Thanks. We're looking at all possibilities." He smiled hesitantly. "What makes you think it was a woman?"

"Because of her figure. She was curvaceous." I used my hands to air outline a figure eight and gave a low whistle.

"I get it." He laughed. "I'd like to have dinner with you... a restaurant this time."

"Sure, I'd like that." I gave him a warm smile and opened the car door.

"One more thing, let's keep this between us. I'll probably be seeing you at the hospital. There are a lot of people still on our list to question. I wouldn't want things to get messed up. Here's my card. Call me with your number."

I took his card, put it in my jacket pocket, and got out of the car. We smiled our good byes and I started up the stairs to my apartment. As I placed my key into the slot I heard his car drive away.

Chapter 8

I plopped on my couch and leaned against the overstuffed cushions. It was about time I called Hector. Jose was lucky to have someone that he could go to with his spiritual questions. I picked up the phone and began dialing. I heard the first ring and then the second ring. I found myself wishing that Hector was my godfather too and was glad when he answered.

"Bendición," I asked Hector for his blessing.

"Santo, mi'ja. Glad to hear from you. Ana was just here. Too bad you missed her. You could have said hi."

Ana was Hector's spiritual running buddy. I met her at the first misa I attended at Jose's place. She and Hector went everywhere together and worked in spiritual rooms throughout the five boroughs of New York City. She was quite a few years his senior but somehow got around as easily as everyone else. He was devoted to her and she taught him everything he knew. They were practically inseparable.

"That's too bad. I would have loved to say hello." I tucked my legs up under me and got into a comfortable position. I knew Hector was busy and got down to business. "I'm still not sleeping so well."

"Did you do those things that I suggested you do? Did you put the glass of water on the floor under your bed?"

"Yes, everything," I answered. "Don't even bother to ask. You know me. I do everything you tell me to do."

I could imagine him in his living room holding the receiver in one hand and a fat Habanos Premium between his teeth looking deeply into the smoke as it curled around him.

"We've been at this a while. I think we should set you up with a misa."

"A misa? Really? Do you think I'm ready?" I was suddenly apprehensive and excited at the same time. The thought of having a spiritual séance was intimidating. Although it wasn't my own, the information I received at Jose's misa was jarring. It seemed everyone knew so much about me and I never met them before in my life. I couldn't even imagine the messages I would receive if the misa was focused on me.

"Sure," he said, "we could have it here at my place."

"Great. It's much roomier there than it is at my place. Who'll be there?"

"I'm sure you're going to have lots of questions." I could practically hear him smiling at the other end of the line. "How about we pick out a day that we're both free and then we can move forward with the details."

"Okay. I'm free on any Sunday. I work some Saturdays."

"Tell me what's going on at that job of yours. Something is, isn't there?

"Definitely is, a doctor was killed."

"Why is your name up in it? You've got to keep your personal business personal."

"I know that... it isn't what you think... whatever that is. I just happened to be working the day that he was found... or really he was found the next morning. He was killed that evening or sometime during the night. They found him early the next morning."

"I saw something about that on the news the other night. I didn't realize that you were involved."

"I'm not involved..."

"Listen to me. You are involved. I see it... look at

your calendar and call me in the morning. We'll make solid plans for the misa. You need this sooner than you think. Maybe I'll get more information on it tonight when I go to sleep."

"Will do. Have a good night." I turned my phone off and decided I wasn't going to spend the night awake ruminating about my possible involvement. I went on a search for Ms. G. and couldn't find her anywhere. When I got under my thick comforter, she appeared from nowhere and jumped up onto my bed, fully expecting me to spoon her.

❀

The staff squeezed into the pews at the Windsor Medical Center Chapel where we waited for the minister to begin the memorial service. There was a poster board on an easel with a collage of pictures that chronicled Dr. Campbell's life set to the side of the podium. The hospital administration, at the urging of the Board of Trustees, had gone through a lot of trouble to have this homage ready merely a few days after his untimely death.

I stood at the back of the chapel. Shadows formed from the pillar that helped me keep distant from it all. Although as Sophia's assistant, I knew that I had to be ready for any unexpected issues or needs that might come up. I watched as Charlotte Campbell, the very rich first Mrs. Campbell, arrived with their twelve-year-old son, Ted. They walked to the first row and took their seats before the collage of photos that painfully reminded them of the man they once knew. Young Ted favored his mother's short stature and ruddy skin. His brown hair fell over his eyes hiding him from the curious stares that the staff didn't attempt to hide. We all watched him grow up and the general feeling was that we needed to continue watching over him, especially now that his father was gone. Ted looked as though he wanted to be anywhere but the inside of a hospital chapel, waiting for his father's memorial service. The child would have been better placed running in the middle of a rugby field or fielding an ice puck while gliding on hockey skates. He leaned his head on his mother's shoulder and she tightened her arm around him.

Their elder son, Charles, had sent word that he would be unable to attend. Charles would attend the family's intimate service at Brooklyn's Greenwood Cemetery that was planned to happen in a couple of days. His mother understood and supported this selfless decision of flying out to Maryland to continue his work on a new surgical technique he was researching and trying to perfect. A promising cardiac surgeon, Charles followed his father's footsteps by entering the medical field. He was quite the opposite of his brother. The family was proud at the physical likeness between Charles and his father and often spoke about how different their personalities were. Unlike his father, Charles barely looked up from his scalpel and his books.

Seeing Dr. Campbell's family left me feeling a little unnerved. It never really crossed my mind at how established he actually was. The way he endlessly flirted with every woman he interacted with gave me the impression that he came from a fractured household. Never did I imagine that he would be the father of someone who already had a reputable medical career. I was a little embarrassed that I'd fallen for him.

I knew better now and had to chalk it up to that little episode being a learning experience for me. My sobriety wasn't just about ditching alcohol. Now, being sober, when I felt lonely, I picked up my phone and called a friend. I went to museums and libraries so often that I even carried a library card in my pocket. The last time I had one was in grammar school. Most importantly, if I found myself struggling I would go to an AA meeting where I could talk about my loneliness. I no longer had to do anything that I might regret.

The organist struck the first chord. The minister walked down the aisle toward the lectern at the front of the altar. The somber music filled the air. At that moment, Dr. Price walked into the chapel. I waited for the fireworks. Although Dr. Campbell believed his wife walked on water, the nurses at the hospital had very different opinions about the chief surgical resident.

Dr. Price was known for making scathing remarks to the nurses about the service that they provided to their clients. She thought nothing of opening up sterile trays and leaving them after use at the patient's bedside, fully expecting a nurse to leave his or her work duties to clean up after her. The most offensive of all acts was when she verbally attacked a nurse in front of an ill client. Other residents and attending physicians tried to be diplomatic when telling her that her behavior was unacceptable but Dr. Price never seemed to care. She continued to do whatever she pleased and seemed insensitive to the feelings or reactions of the persons that she offended.

Dr. Price wore her very long dark hair up at the nape of her neck. The only time anyone would get a glimpse of her glorious strands was when she was at a cocktail party or reception. Seeing her pale flawless skin up close reminded me of how much she looked like a vampire. I shook my head a bit. I had to get those cobwebs out. Be present. 'Mocus,' mostly out of focus, was not the way I wanted to be.

My thoughts wandered to the newlywed's brownstone. Sophia had me drop over a few personal items from Dr. C.'s office as well as some papers for Price to sign. I remember looking at the structure thinking that it was the size of a mansion. They had much of it gutted but saved the ornate ceiling and the antique woodwork was restored to its original splendor. I couldn't help notice the vast difference to Marge's home that was located only a few blocks away.

Allie walked towards me from the doorway. "Hi," she whispered. "I'm sorry I'm so late. I had a patient that was taking the longest to wake up from anesthesia." Allie gave me a quick hug and kiss. "Everyone else is here already. We practically closed up shop in order to be here for the memorial." We were getting closer because of this tragedy.

I couldn't help but call the situation as I saw it. "This is a nightmare. Look, at the front of the church. Not only is Doctor Price sitting up there but look to the left. There's his ex-wife, Charlotte Campbell, and one of his sons."

Allie's jaw tightened. "What was it with that guy? I guess the fact that he was pretty well respected as a surgeon is the only thing that he had going. His personal life was a mess."

"It makes me uncomfortable... but anyone can date, anyone can get married more than once. There really isn't any shame in that. I mean... is there?"

"No, I guess not." She seemed on the verge of tears. "I hate to be judgmental. It's just that... well, he was with so many of the nurses here..."

"Allie, you?" I tugged at her sleeve. It wasn't my business but I couldn't help but ask. Otherwise why would she be so upset? "No... don't tell me, you and Doctor C..."

"Of course not." Allie straightened up. "What are you thinking?"

"Hey, anything is possible. He was a good looking guy. Quite charming as well."

"Ya think?" She suddenly sounded like a tough cookie. "He was a predator. No one was safe around him."

"Come on, we're all big boys and girls," I said. "Even I know that. Shhh, let's be quiet. They're just about to start the service."

We sat back and listened to the clerk, Ms. Cowan, from Central Supply, who began singing a solo accompanied only by the organ. I felt as if I'd been transported to a gospel church, her voice was so soulful. The chapel was overflowing at this point. Many of the attendees sat there with their eyes closed. Once Ms. Cowan finished the song, Reverend Samm, who had conducted special services at the hospital before, began his speech. Unlike the other services I'd previously attended, I realized there wasn't going to be a regular service or prayers at this memorial. The plan was to give the opportunity to everyone to share their feelings about Dr. Campbell.

"Anyone who would like to say a few words about our Doctor Campbell will have the opportunity to do so today."

The C.E.O. got up from his front row seat. "I'd like to extend my heart-felt sympathy to the Campbell family who we are honored to have here today. His was a person beyond compare. It's not often that a hospital can brag about having a renowned surgeon on staff that is also a two time runner in the Boston Marathon. We are blessed and fortunate that he is part of our family..."

I heard the C.E.O. slip into using the present tense when describing Dr. Campbell and I realized it would take time before the community got used to the fact that he was gone. I couldn't help but notice that there were more than two sets of eyes whose mascara was spreading down blushed cheeks. I continued listening as a line of mourners formed in order to pay their respects to the surgeon.

After the memorial, Allie and I linked arms and went to sit in the hospital's atrium. We wanted to reorganize ourselves before going back to work. We sat on a leather bench in front of cacti that extended several feet up to the ceiling. The bromeliads surrounding them were exotic and surprising in their beauty. The natural cups in the middle of the large leaves held gorgeous dark pink buds. The tropical garden reminded me that I kept meaning to ask Marge if I could do some work in her garden. It had the residuals of something beautiful but no one had worked in it for a long time.

"I have to share something with you," Allie said. "I didn't want to tell you anything before because, well, I don't want to get into more trouble than I'm already in."

"Go ahead; at this point I wouldn't be surprised at anything at all."

"I might lose my job."

"What are you talking about? Since when? What's going on?"

"They're saying I didn't lock up the O.R. suite the night Doctor Campbell was murdered."

What I was hearing from Allie was so crazy. "What does that mean? That his murder is your fault? Are you responsible for locking up?"

"I thought I had locked the outer doors before we left. I've wanted to ask you; do you remember if I did?"

"No, all I remember is saying good night to Jimmy. He was still there, buffing, wasn't he?"

Allie let out a deep sigh. "You remember exactly what I do. I'm the person usually responsible for locking the outer doors. There was so much commotion with the code going on. Remember, that turned out to be a false alarm. There were a lot more staff people there than usual because of it."

"But how are you responsible if Jimmy has keys… they have to do the maintenance during the evening. There are too many people around during the day for them to tackle that kind of work."

"I think they're looking for someone to be their fall guy and that person might be me. We left a bit later because of the false code and Jimmy was there earlier. It was just a slight change in the usual protocol."

"But did they say that you're actually going to lose your job? I would think that Security should be making their rounds."

"It's a possibility… I have an appointment with the union rep. I'll ask him about that detail. The administration is planning to have a meeting about this early next week."

"You mean, Sophia and Mister Donaldson." I shook my head. "I swear I didn't know anything about this. They probably kept it quiet since we're friends."

"Please, if you hear anything, anything at all, let me know."

"I promise…"

Just as I was reassuring Allie, the atrium door swung open. Charlotte and Ted Campbell walked in. Ted's eyes were reddened as he spoke passionately to his mother. They were across the room and it was impossible to hear what he was saying through the dense foliage. It was obvious that she didn't want anyone to hear what they were talking about, but his tears and her clenched lips spoke volumes. The former surgeon's wife took a tissue out of her bag and wiped at his face, she looked over her shoulder, and then straightened his school-boy tie. They left the room as quickly as they had entered.

"What do you think is going on?" I leaned forward

on the leather settee.

"I know less and less each moment. I don't know how I'm going to survive this."

"Allie, you're exaggerating. You're not going to lose your job."

"If only..." Allie stood up. "We'll talk later. Thanks."

I watched my friend leave the atrium. I never saw her look so sad in all the years that we worked at Windsor. Something had definitely turned sour.

Chapter 9

Later that afternoon, I was flabbergasted by Sophia's news. "You'll be going to Puerto Rico after all. There's no way Mister Donaldson can afford to leave the hospital while it's in the throes of an unsolved murder. His secretary won't be going either. That leaves us and Todd Roberts from the Education and Research department to make the presentation in Rincón," she said, rapidly flipping through papers while sitting at her desk. "Do you think you can be ready at such short notice?" Sophia scrutinized me over her half-moon eyeglasses.

"Yes, it won't be any problem at all." I tried hard to contain my excitement. Jose had been on target, as usual, when he suggested I keep my summer things out. "All I have to do is throw a few pieces into my luggage and I'm good to go. I'm an easy traveler."

"Good. By the way, I'll need your help with my dogs. I'm bringing them with me."

"No problem. It'll be fun having them. I'll walk them on the beach…"

Sophia waved her hand. "Please contact Detective Rodriguez; he wanted me to confirm when I'd be leaving. Let him know about our change in plans."

"Sure thing, right away."

This made things even better. I didn't have the nerve to call him even though I was walking around with his card in my bag wherever I went. I would take it out at night and place it next to my phone, then put it back in my bag each morning. This would be the perfect reason for me to call him. I was a little worried after that night. Even though he seemed to understand where I was coming from when I told him about the dream, I was reluctant to call

85

him. I had a feeling he wasn't as into my premonition as he led me to believe. I walked back to my desk and dialed his number from my cell phone and got his voice mail. This made it even easier. He had to call me back now and the fact I used my cell phone to leave him my number made it easier for him to do so. Nice.

❦

The weekend carrier seemed to be the perfect size for the conference. As I packed I thought about my father and decided to call him. It had been a few weeks since we last spoke. Our relationship was improving but there was still a lot more to work through. He sounded happy to hear me and I was glad I called. My mother was totally indifferent and it would take much more than a few months of sobriety to get me through that hurdle. I could just hear my father begging, "Reina, it's your daughter" and my mother saying, "¿Y que? So what, Octavio, you know your daughter." My father tried to get my attention through the line. I focused on him, it was exciting news that I had to share and I knew he would be happy to hear it.

"I found out today that I'm going to Puerto Rico on business. Can you imagine? I'll be leaving on Monday. We're going to be on the western side of the island." I began sorting through a pile of underwear that I planned on packing.

"Aguada?" He sounded doubtful through the phone. "Are you serious? They're going to have a business conference in Aguada?"

"No, not Aguada, Rincón." I couldn't wait to get there. My wish for a vacation, even a couple of days long, was being granted.

"I'll give you your Tía Minerva's phone number. She'll be happy to see you. She always loved you."

"That's great, Dad," I said. "I didn't know that." Sometimes he was so frustrating. Why didn't he say anything like this before? It's always good to know that someone loves you even if you feel as if you don't love yourself.

"You were just like her when you were growing up. She used to call you her brujita- her little witch."

"Wait, I never heard this before, what do you mean, brujita, the little witch?"

He laughed. "I'm not sure... it probably had to do with the fact that there were misas at our house on Saturdays and then on Sundays the women in our family would sit in church with their heads covered with mantillas. But that was a long time ago. You know, mums the word. I'm not sure what they do there now. It's been years since any one of us have been there."

The whole thing was amazing. He was telling me pretty much the same thing that Rod had said about his family the other night. My father had also experienced misas. To think that it almost skipped a generation.

"You were probably about three. You were a talker... talk, talk, talk," Octavio reminisced. "Your great Tía Lola was still alive. She loved you to death. Funny, I forgot all about that. So, when did you say you were going?"

"Monday," I said. "But please, tell me more, don't stop now. Why did she say I was a witch?" I knew deep inside that there was something different about me and this confirmed it. I tried to imagine myself at the age of three.

"You two just seemed to get along. She said that you had the sight. That you could see more than Doña Margó... now that lady had the gift."

"Why have you been holding out on me?" I couldn't help but ask. It seemed a chunk of my history had been missing. "Who was Doña Margó?"

"She lived in Atalaya, one of the barrios. If she's alive, she's got to be ancient. That lady could tell you what you had for lunch two days ago and who slept in your bed the night before that. I used to think that she was more of a gossip than a witch."

"I always wanted to be like that…"

"You were."

I sighed. If only I took care of myself better than I did. It was only recently that I started meditating after Hector made the suggestion. According to him, it was one way to open up my channels.

"Your aunt also called you 'la gitana'," my father added, "and said that you were gonna be a fortune teller, like a gypsy woman or something. I guess she was wrong."

"Not completely," I admitted. "I'm not a fortune teller but I do read the cards. Tarot."

"Once you let that stuff out, there's no going back."

"Come on, Dad, I'm not sixteen and we're not talking about Ouija boards. This is serious stuff we're talking about." I was attracted to the psychic spiritual world and wondered what my father would say if he knew I was thinking about receiving beads in the Orisha tradition. Spiritual and religious paths were opening for me and I would love for him to know more about my growing passions.

"Your mother would have a heart attack if she heard you talk about this. I guess it skipped a generation," Octavio said with a laugh. "Because your mother sure doesn't have the gift."

I tried to imagine having this talk with my mother. Impossible for many reasons, mostly because we were barely on speaking terms.

"You still there?"

"Yeah, I'm here." The phrase 'Time takes time' flashed across my mind.

Octavio laughed again. "Cheer up, kid. I know what you're thinking. Hold on while I get your aunt's phone number. I'll be right back. Do you want me to put your mother on while you wait? She's right here." I could hear him put his hand over the phone in a poor attempt to muffle what was being said. Still, I heard her refusing to speak to me and it stung a little bit. "Oh, never mind, she's running out to the store. Hold on."

I was glad he couldn't see me rolling my eyes. My mother was probably going to the corner liquor store to buy her daily pint of blackberry brandy. Ugh. I tried to shake the nauseated feeling off. It was none of my business. All I could do was pray for her. I had enough to deal with my own recovery than to worry about her continued addiction.

"Okay, here it is. Ready?" My dad was back on the line. After giving me the number, we spoke about a budín de pan, a bread pudding recipe that I had asked for a month earlier.

"Don't worry about it. I guess we've all been busy."

"Drop on over when you come back from your trip, I'd love to see you," he said. "In fact, I'll make you the budín myself."

"I'll think about it." I couldn't commit. While I wanted to see my father, I wasn't sure if I was up for a visit there yet. "We'll see. Love you, bye."

Hanging up, I felt a sadness that I used to mistake for rage during my foggy days and knew that I just had to do the next right thing. I got back to the shorts and beach tops that were waiting to be folded. I had to live in the day, not worry about yesterday, or fret about tomorrow.

Chapter 10

Standing at the top of the airplane steps, I could feel my wavy hairline immediately turn into ringlets. The humidity blasted us and the suit jacket that was completely comfortable in New York was way too heavy under the balmy tropical air. I looked around as I felt my clothes starting to stick to my skin and noticed that some of the other passengers were wearing white and breezy loose clothing. Had they actually boarded in J.F.K. wearing those light garments? I wondered if they were already on vacation mode. I couldn't wait to get under a cool shower or jump into a turquoise blue swimming pool.

"Arf, arf!"

Sophia struggled with her overnight bag, the two barking dogs, and a small piece of rolling luggage. The antihistamine tablets we'd given the dogs to quiet them down for the three-and-a-half-hour trip had worn off too early and they were acting up. They weren't doing well around strangers and their little bodies needed to stretch after being held captive in their Sherpa lined bags.

"Here, let me help you," I offered. "I can take one of them."

The amber light on the conveyor belt lit and the alarm went off signaling the suitcases were coming around. We stood side by side with the lines of others who were also waiting for their luggage.

"Sophia, on second thought, why don't you take the dogs for a walk and I'll get the luggage."

"Okay, if you don't mind," Sophia agreed and began walking the dogs to the double doors that led out to both the street and parking lot. She turned back for a moment. "Maybe next time you can bring your suitcase on the plane like I did. This way we wouldn't have to wait for the handlers to bring them here. We could have been in a cab by now."

"Sure, Sophia, maybe next time." I had to smile to myself. The woman was clearly not seeing the facts but it wasn't my place to correct her. It wasn't harming anyone if I let her think that her idea was the better one- no matter what. My job was hard to come by and the benefits were generous. It wasn't worth losing over a couple of extra bags. Any one of my co-workers would have given their eye teeth for my position.

The baggage carousel made complete rotations a few times. A rose colored bag kept popping up. Where the heck was my bag? My nerves were starting to get to me when I finally spotted it. I stuck my arm out and grabbed at the handle without needing to check the identification tag, I knew it was mine. The leopard-like design was unique. Except for that pink one, everyone else seemed to have the uniform black bag. Pulling it off the conveyor, I felt a stir of excitement in my chest. It was finally time to begin my long awaited trip.

Once outside, we were led to a shuttle bus that would take us to the resort. Large fruit bearing trees and a golf course were a welcomed sight as we headed off the small airport that was adjacent to a military base. A few people were jogging and some were playing at the tennis courts that were visible from the main street. The shuttle drove a couple of miles through small towns that boasted with souvenir shops, variety stores, outdoor restaurants, and haute couture evening gowns. We eventually passed a road sign that named the area as '*Crash Boat*.' The ocean vista conspired with the sky to match its clear sapphire tones. Tall palm trees dotted the beach. The horizon went as far as our eyes could take us.

We continued the ride through the villages that were framed by the endless ocean and I was glad the driver decided to take the scenic route. There was an autopista, a highway, that ran the length of the isla but he thought we'd enjoy seeing what otherwise would have remained invisible to us as tourists. The ride from the airport was a bit longer than expected but it was so worth it.

Finally arriving at the resort, that looked exactly like the website had promised, we got out and I took a long stretch. As we gathered the keys to our respective suites, Sophia and I agreed to meet for dinner that evening. It was a relief knowing that we were separated.

The villas were tiny secluded living quarters that included a master bedroom and bath. Because of the privacy between dwellings, Sophia would have her shaggy babies with her but they wouldn't be within earshot of the other guests. Each suite had an elegantly furnished living room that led to a private pool overlooking the ocean. The foliage that surrounded the individual villas muffled any noise. A path surrounding the pool led to the common road that guided us to the beach. It was the first place I had ever been where there were private outdoor showers. The place was magnificent.

Instead of going to the pool, I eased myself onto the bed thinking that a short nap couldn't hurt. Waking up at three in the morning to catch my flight left me exhausted. It seemed that I had just laid my head on the pillow when the phone on my nightstand began to ring. I opened my eyes and picked up the receiver.

"Your party is at the bar awaiting your arrival, Miss Muñiz." I heard a heavily accented male voice on the line.

"Thank you."

I looked at the clock that marked 7:00 p.m. and was amazed that I had spent most of the afternoon asleep. I took a shower in a hurry and got dressed. Before leaving the room I checked myself out in the mirror. 'To thine own self be true' rang in my head. I hadn't looked for any meetings in the area and forgot to ask the concierge for one. Not good, but I'd been so busy with the trip preparations and the crazy goings on at the hospital that I kept putting it off, until I completely forgot to check for any. While I didn't feel a desire to drink, it was always a feat saying that to others at bars that seemed to take extraordinary pleasure in trying to ply me with cocktails.

Finding my way to the bar, I saw that Todd, Sophia, and a couple of administrators from other area hospitals and medical centers on the mainland were waiting for me.

"Great, Daisy, you're here," Todd said. He wore a flowery shirt that reminded me of something my father wore in the seventies. "I thought you floated out to sea." He held a mojito in his hand.

"Where were you?" Sophia glowed in her bright tropical outfit. "I wanted to go over the presentation planning with you at some point today."

"I'm sorry. I'd thought we agreed to meet for dinner. It didn't occur to me."

"That's okay," Todd advised her. "We can double up in the morning…"

"We have the rest of the evening. I'd be willing to meet right after dinner. There are a couple of work rooms I'm sure that we could use."

"Listen to the little lady." He sipped his mojito. "Serious girl, aren't you? We'll have none of that tonight. All too rare to be in the tropics, isn't it, Sophia?"

"I'm willing to work too, if you are." Sophia looked expectantly at him. "We can surely meet right after dinner. I believe I'm as rested as Daisy seems to be."

"We'll meet for a onceover tomorrow. Our

presentation isn't until two. One should never mix business with pleasure and tonight is pleasure, ladies." Todd called the bartender over and asked what the rest of us at the table were ordering. Everyone at the table ordered a drink except for one man from Oklahoma who said he would stick to seltzer or mineral water.

"I think I'll just have a diet cola," I said.

Todd might have been the Director of Education and Research but he was a bore. I knew he had no intention of attending any of the conference sessions or workshops but our own. He would probably set up a desk at the bar if he could. That last gentleman helped me to stick to my resolve and not have a mojito just to get along with the rest of the group. I nodded at him and lifted my glass of soda to him when it arrived.

The group ordered local cuisine. The arroz con habichuelas, the mofongo, and the bacalao were to die for and everyone loved the avocado salad. Only a couple of folks could stomach the thought of the ensalada de pulpo. One of my father's specialties was creating wonderful octopus salads, so I was glad to eat it.

At the end of the spectacular meal, a few in the group decided to stay to throw back a few more drinks. I was about to excuse myself when the Midwestern man came over and quietly spoke to me.

"I see you only drank a cola," he said. "Are you a friend of Bill's?"

I laughed when I remembered how I reacted the first time I heard that term. Who in the world was Bill? Bill Wilson was the founder of Alcoholics Anonymous. Saying you're a friend of Bill's was a way to recognize those in recovery without being too intrusive about it. Today I was proud to be called his friend. "Yes, I am. Don't mind me. It's a joke that wasn't that funny to begin with. I'm Daisy."

I shook the man's hand.

"I'm Dan," he said. "I thought dinner would never end. There's a late night meeting we could go to down the road. It's at a church."

"Aren't they all? I'm game. It's so dark out there. I'd be happy to go with you."

"It's heavily guarded around here," Dan said. "We got in early last night and I took a walk to the beach. There were quite a few uniformed officers around. I guess they want to protect the clientele. I have no issue with that."

"Neither do I," I said. "Let's go."

We walked out of the resort gates and strolled a few hundred yards toward the church. Once we arrived we saw that there were quite a number of people outside preparing to enter the church for the meeting. I felt like I was at home and as if I had never left Brooklyn. There were quite a few English-speaking meeting goers and I enjoyed what turned out to be a bilingual meeting. I was reminded by the shares that nothing was worth a drink or losing the recovery I worked so hard on attaining. Some people could drink and some people couldn't. The way my life had turned out, it proved to me that I belonged to the 'couldn't drink' group.

After the meeting, we returned to the resort and said our good nights in the lobby. I passed the lounge and saw Todd laughing with some of the other attendees. All were obviously having a great time. So was I, but in a different sort of way. As I walked away from the colorful scene of my colleagues, I thought about my plans for the next evening. I would be connecting with family I hadn't seen in years. I yawned as I made my way toward my personal tiny villa. Who would have ever thought that I'd be in Puerto Rico on business? Life was good.

"Daisy!" the voice called out to me just as it did in Brooklyn. This time it seemed to be carried by the waves of the ocean. A dog barked from somewhere in the distance. Sitting up, I shook with a chill that shot through my body. The room was warm and humid. I passed on turning on the air conditioner knowing that the heat was a gift that I wanted to take advantage of before returning to the coming harsh winter of New York City. I was sure that I wouldn't have this opportunity again in a very long time.

The clock showed it was three in the morning. It had been a few days since this happened and I began to wonder why now. Why in Puerto Rico and not the last week in Brooklyn?

"I'm here," I spoke aloud to the breeze coming in through the double glass doors that I left open. I rummaged through my briefcase and found the pen and legal pad I planned to use in a few short hours. "I'm going to sit here and listen. I'm going to write down all the thoughts that go through my head. I know that those thoughts will be the things that you want me to know."

Hoping this maneuver would work, I tried to clear my mind and allow whatever thoughts to filter through. Not knowing if it would work for sure I sat and waited. Nothing seemed to come through. Instead of wrestling with my blank brain I decided to go out for a walk. It was late but according to Dan, there were multiple security guards patrolling the grounds.

Pulling on my shorts, tee shirt, and slipping on a pair of flip flops, I went out. It was a glorious, sultry night. The air was thick and I could smell the heavy perfume from the flowered bushes that surrounded the pool. I hadn't thought to ask what they were that afternoon but the fragrance seemed to be stronger now than earlier.

The beach waves pulled me to come closer to the

shore. I felt like I was in a dream. The rhythmical lapping sounds were lulling to my whole being. The deep indigo blue of the ocean matched the color of the night sky. I remembered what Hector told me when Jose was initiated. He said that the goddess of the waters, Yemayá, would always be with me, providing me with solace and healing. Tonight, I began to feel that at a personal level, without all the ceremony and people dancing to the drums as they worshipped the Orisha at Jose's tambor. This was for me to experience alone, simply, and I was enthralled by the feeling of being awake and alive. I dipped my toes into the foamy shore waters. The warmth surprised me and I waded in just a bit further to my knees. I received a feeling of liberation that I hadn't really ever experienced before.

After a while I backed away from the water and sat at the shoreline. At first I was a bit fearful of being outside by myself with no one in sight but then reminded myself that the grounds and beach of the resort were protected. I closed my eyes and sank down into the warm sand. Was there a time that I ever felt so relaxed? If there was, I didn't remember it. Not by myself anyway. I was so used to finding something to do and someone had to be with me. I was always on the hunt looking for a way to get rid of the prickles. I sat at the shore reveling in this desired solitude. Ultimately, my left brain kicked in and reminded me that I had meetings to attend in the morning.

Sauntering back to my quarters, I took a warm outdoor shower before crawling underneath the covers. Without having to share my bed with Ms. G., I stretched out and promptly fell asleep in the middle of a yawn.

Chapter 11

The presentation went off without a hitch, just as I knew that it would. I was excited and relieved to leave the grounds. One of Sophia's dogs was having a poor reaction to the sweltering heat and lay there exhausted after a brief attempt at a walk. Sophia was annoyed at Todd who made no effort to sit on the panel as planned. She had to field all the questions regarding the hospital's recidivism rates that were lower than the national average. The audience was extremely responsive to the talk and while we had all the facts, knowing Todd had come along for the ride rankled at Sophia. This exasperation trickled on down to me but I decided to zip the lip and made a call to my aunt's house to have someone pick me up as soon as the day's seminar was over. I had just enough time to wiggle out of my suit and put on the gauzy yellow dress I bought at the resort boutique. Soon, I'd see my family and I couldn't wait.

Too excited to sit down, I stood in the front lobby when a tall brown-skinned male with tight curly hair climbed out of a small patched-up Toyota that pulled up to the curb. He walked over to me with his hand extended.

"Daisy?"

"Yes. Felix?" I held out my hand for a shake, but my cousin opened his arms and hugged me, giving me a kiss on the cheek. He was a few years older than me and we only met once when I was three years old. Since I had absolutely no memory of that visit, this was our first meeting as far as I was concerned. "Do you speak English?"

"Yes, I went to high school in Florida." He pointed to my handbag. "Where's your luggage?"

"Oh, no, I'm not planning to stay. I'm here for a

short trip and can only stay the evening. We're headed back to New York tomorrow afternoon."

"Oh, Mami's going to be upset." Felix scratched the back of his head. "She's got the extra room ready for you."

"A short visit, that's all I can make," I repeated "I'm here for work but I didn't want to pass up meeting everybody."

"So you don't remember the last time you were here?" We climbed into the car and he quickly edged out onto the road. "You were very little. I showed you the horse we had in the back of the house."

"No memory of that." I shook my head. "My father reminded me about our Tía Lola. Do you remember her?"

"Of course, Tía died a couple of years ago," he said. "She was great."

"I heard she was special." I hoped he knew what I meant and keep the conversation going.

"She could tell you things that were going to happen before they did."

"What a loss for me," I said. "I wish I had gotten to know her. My father said that I was just like her."

"You mean seeing things?" He laughed. "Don't say that too loud around here. People get spooked easily. Nobody wants to talk about it. Taboo, you know."

"I heard that. I wonder why?"

"It's a very spiritual place… you know how it is," he tried to explain. "The people here are good and like to lead simple lives. They don't want to stir anything up. My mother will tell you more about it. You have a lot in common with her. You'll see."

I felt a stirring of understanding between us. By the look in his eye I knew that he was very spiritual too. I gazed out the window as we passed the palm trees that lined the streets. For years I felt slightly different from my family members in New York. Twenty minutes into meeting my cousin and I felt like I finally met my true family. It was weird the way things like that happened.

Felix pulled over into the driveway of one of the houses. They were all designed differently and each was painted a beautiful tropical hue; turquoise, yellow, coral, and pink. Their house was one of the coral ones. It had well-tended shrubs dotting the driveway to the car port. The louver windows were slightly open. The screened door was opened by a tiny plump woman who ran out and drew me into a warm embrace.

"Come in! You are so beautiful!" Tía Minerva said looking at me from head to toe. "You're a grown lady now."

My aunt's welcome was filled with love as she led me into the balcón. It was furnished very sparely. My aunt pointed to a cane rocker and I sat down. Aside from that chair there was a matching cane settee and an easy chair where my aunt sat positively glowing at me. My cousin pulled a folding chair out and made himself comfortable. A couple of low tables were covered with mantillas made of fine lace. One of the tables was a lacquer tray that held a frosted pitcher filled with passion fruit juice.

"¿Jugo de parcha?" she asked, ready to pour.

"Yes, thank you." I accepted the glass and drank. The juice was delicious.

In the corner of the balcony was a statue of an Indian warrior. There was a small cup of black coffee and a cigar placed on the floor in front of it. I couldn't take my eyes off of it.

"He guards the place for me." Titi couldn't help but notice my attraction. "No one who doesn't belong here gets in. He protects us," she said, carefully observing to see how I would react to her words.

"I have friends who do this," I said. "I'm kind of learning too…"

"Good, so it's not strange. Come in to the kitchen. I made some lunch, are you hungry?"

❁

About an hour later, I sat there licking the cream cheese topping off the rich pumpkin dessert they made with me in mind. I was full and satisfied but it wasn't just the food, it was more about having an afternoon with family who, unfortunately, I had almost forgotten about. I wasn't sure how I'd get back to the villa that evening, they'd have to roll me out of the door. This was another type of relaxed feeling that was brand new to me. I decided to try to find out a bit more about my great aunt Lola before I returned.

"I was hoping to hear about Tía Lola," I ventured forth. "Papi told me that I was like her..."

Tía Minerva tilted her head to the side and laughed. "I guess you do look a little like her. She was about a foot shorter than you though."

"Do you have any pictures?" I hadn't thought about the fact that we might actually look like each other.

"Felix, bring me the box." Titi pointed to a heavy wooden armoire in the corner of the living room.

I was speechless when she opened the box. It was filled with black and white photos and some color ones too. I never saw any like these at home. Why hadn't my parents taken any pictures, I wondered?

"This is your Tía Lola when she was a teenager. Yes, you do look a lot like her, now that I see you next to the pictures. I see what Octavio meant."

"Here's your father. This one is of me and him." My aunt scattered a few of them on the table. "Look at this one. You wouldn't believe it. It's your father and your mother when they were first dating, before he went to Viet Nam." Tía Minerva rubbed at her arms. "He looks so happy. I never saw him look like that again. He came back like he'd seen death itself."

"Why do you say that?"

"The men who went to that war..." her voice trailed. "But then he had another problem after a while."

"What are you talking about? What problem?"

"It's better not to talk about it." Her lips seemed to thin out before my eyes. "We have to go on with our lives. These pictures were taken years ago. We were different people then."

"How do you mean, different?" I didn't want her to stop talking. If only she'd go on forever. She was right. The people in these pictures bore no resemblance to my parents. My mother looked so soft in the pictures.

"Did your mother ever talk to you about what happened?" she asked. I could see that she didn't want to give something away that wasn't hers to give.

"If you mean about my brother... I know about that." I found out about him during the first misa I went to and approached my parents about it. They never volunteered any information to me. Once I brought it up my mother had flown into a rage. How dare I bring something up that they'd spent almost thirty years hiding?

"I know that he got hit by a car and my parents were never the same after he died."

"I thought your father was bad after Viet Nam... when your brother died, your father turned into a shadow of the man he used to be but I can't blame him." My aunt gave a quick glance to my cousin and I saw how fiercely proud she was of him. "But then things changed when they had you. They were so happy when you were born."

I was born about three years after my brother was

killed. My mother never forgave my father for being, how she described, 'out of it' and not holding on to his son. She blamed him. That was a discussion I needed to have with my parents. At least, that's what I believed I had to do based on my conversations with my sponsor, Angela.

"I guess they were." I smiled and went through more of the pictures. I was determined to keep things light and also wanted to know more about my great aunt. "Tell me about Tía Lola."

"Too bad you never got to see her in action." Titi Minerva nodded. "That woman could read you in an instant."

"So, she was psychic?"

"Spiritual, is what we call it. Yes. People came to her for readings all the time. She taught me a lot, some I was born with but there was a lot she taught me."

"You mean that people came to you for readings too?"

"Yes, they still line up, well, not really, but they know that I'll see them on Thursdays and Saturdays and they come."

"I want to do that too." The words seemed to fly out of my mouth. "I hear things, is that what happens to you?"

"Yes, and you'll see, the longer you do this the more you'll experience," Tía said. "You'll learn to see clearly. Do you have someone to teach you?"

"Hector, an old friend of mine, is helping but sometimes I wonder. I think that what I'm experiencing isn't normal. No one at home ever talks about it. I think I'm crazy because sometimes I hear voices. At least my ex used to tell me that."

"As long as they're not telling you to hurt someone or are making you sick. If it's not bothering you then I think that in our family, it's normal." Both Minerva and

Felix laughed. "Very normal."

"How come my father wasn't in on this?" I asked. "You all grew up together didn't you?"

"Our father was a strange man. He didn't want to believe. Papá used to say it made us lower class. I think he spent a lifetime trying to hide the fact that he was the same way and he came down hard on your father the few times he seemed interested. On the other hand, our mother had a tight hold on us, as the girls in the house. Even though your father might have been open to this, Papá never allowed him to express it."

"Then how come you're in on it?" I addressed my cousin who was quiet for most of the conversation.

"It was different by that time," he said. "My grandfather died and my father wasn't around too much. I was basically raised by my mother."

"Don't forget that times change, too, mi'ja," Tia Minerva said gently. "Remember that. Your mother could change too."

"Wait, how did you... know anything about my mother?" She caught me off guard with that one.

"She's my comay. I know her since she was that little girl in that picture there. Sometimes life is hard for some of us. Give your mother a chance. That's all I'm saying." Tía reached over to the platter. "Now, don't let this go to waste. Eat."

❦

I curled up on the recliner near the pool when I got back to the resort. It was cooler out and the humidity had dropped. I wrapped a shawl around my shoulders and thought about my mother. Based on how she acted it seemed like she might never change. My own ability to change was what would make the difference in my life. Tía

Minerva's words struck a chord of hope that was deep within me. All I could do was my part and pray that my mother would also do hers. My father had changed a lot after we had the talk about my brother. He was finally open to going to a therapist and wasn't as distant as he had been when I was growing up. The psychiatrist said he suffered from Post Traumatic Stress Disorder from being on active duty during a terrible war and it worsened when my brother was killed.

Practically everything had been a secret when I was growing up and I couldn't figure out why it had to be that way. Even when it came to being psychic or 'spiritual' like they called it. Was it such a horrible thing to see through the veils? What was wrong with being a witch? Would I be a good witch or a bad witch? I laughed to myself imagining Glinda, the good witch of the south. She seemed to think it made a difference. Would I prefer cauldrons to wands? I began to doze when I heard a knocking.

"Daisy, wake up…please!" Sophia called through the door. "Dear, you must wake up!"

I walked over to the glass enclosure and slid it aside. "Is something wrong?" My head felt as if it was stuffed with cotton. I must have fallen into a deep sleep at the pool.

"Yes, I have some bad news," she said. "Sit down."

We went into the sitting room and I perched on the couch. Sophia sat next to me.

She placed her hand over mine. "Doctor Price is dead."

It was as though someone had poured ice cold water over me as her words took form in my mind. Sophia's appearance had also changed. The skin around her eyes was dark. It was obvious that she was under strain. That, combined with her not wearing make-up, showed how distraught she was over this.

"Wow." I had no other words to convey what I was feeling.

"It seems they found her dead in her house," Sophia explained. "Donaldson just contacted me. She didn't show up for a scheduled surgery. One of the other surgeons pitched in for her. They figured she finally let herself get some sleep."

Todd stepped into view and chimed in, "She had ridiculously high standards. Everyone told her to take time off. She refused." The smell of scotch emanated from him and it burned at my nostrils.

Sophia warded him off with a curt wave. "When she missed rounds in the afternoon, everyone became very worried. They tried calling her but there was no answer. Doctor Stevens went over to her house. He saw a couple of days' worth of mail on the floor in the vestibule. Thank goodness for those glass doors. He figured that she hadn't been out and tried the phone again. When she didn't respond, he called the police."

I kept my hand over my mouth. I was stuck between wanting to say something, anything, and feeling slightly queasy. First Doctor Campbell was dead and now his wife. They were just married. I finally managed to speak. "How did she die?"

"They're not sure yet," Sophia said. "There's going to be an emergency autopsy. They'll have the report in a couple of days."

"What does this do to the investigation?" I asked. "Do they think she was murdered?

Sophia and Todd looked at each other. Sophia turned to me. "It's very possible that it was suicide."

"Suicide! Doctor Price?" I was aghast at the thought. "Why would anyone think of that? She wasn't the type."

"What I'm going to tell you must stay in the strictest of all confidences. Do you understand?"

"Yes, of course." I moved to the edge of the couch closer to Sophia. "You have to know that you can trust me by now."

"Doctor Price has made several suicide attempts," Sophia said. "Doctor Campbell tried to end their relationship several times but she refused. He once told me that she said she'd prefer to die than not have him in her life."

"You've got to be kidding me." A throbbing started at my temples. "This is all too much to take in, I'm sorry. I don't know why I'm so upset by this."

Todd held out a bottle of scotch he'd apparently been carrying and went over to the bar. He poured some of the amber liquid into a glass and tried to hand it to me. "Here, drink this."

I stood up and pushed the glass away gently. "No, thank you, I'm okay, really. It's just unexpected." I went into the pocket sized kitchenette and poured myself a glass of water from the tap. "I want to stay clearheaded. You understand, don't you?"

"Yes, of course." He followed me and put his hand on my shoulder. "I like to be just as present for Sophia as you are." He sipped at his glass.

If that was how to keep the heat off so he wouldn't push me toward a drink, I was fine with it. Being so close to alcohol after so long was as repulsing as it was tempting. Here in Puerto Rico no one would know if I had one drink to calm down after receiving this awful news. Dr. Price wasn't the type of person that anyone could get close to but, still, another life was gone.

I walked back into the living room. "Would you two

mind excusing me for a couple of minutes? I can meet you at your room, Sophia, in a bit. Is that okay with you?"

I opened the door before they had a chance to register what I said. I needed some time to process this. Everyone in my support team advised me to call them whenever I needed to and that it didn't matter if it was three o'clock in the morning or three o'clock in the afternoon. This was my opportunity to test it. It took me a minute to decide who that person would be. Letty was my first choice. The problem with my calling her was Mike. He'd complain for days if he was home. He might be away on a case but I didn't want to upset the apple cart. Things had just become a little smoother for them. Allie was my second choice but telling her might actually be a disaster. Calling my sponsor, Angela, was not something that I particularly wanted to do. We weren't close, that was the truth of it, but I knew the old saying, 'better to save your ass than your face.' Some of those sayings sounded awful but they worked if one paid attention to them.

There was no answer but I left a message anyway. "Angela, I hate to call you in the middle of the night. I'm in Puerto Rico and had a glass of scotch about an inch from my nose. Since I don't want to drink, I'm calling you instead of taking that glass. Sorry I missed you. I'll call you again when I can. I'm with my boss. I'll be all right. I am not going to drink and that's a promise to myself."

I took a deep breath as I turned off my phone. Seeing no one, I went to Sophia's villa and knocked on the door. Todd opened the door.

"What got into you?" he asked. "You kind of threw us out." Todd stood about a foot too close to me and his eyes were bloodshot. He was about nine-tenths into a quart.

"Sorry if it seemed like that. I was asleep when you came over. I needed to wash my face." I pulled my orange and yellow silk shawl close around my shoulders. "It's a bit chilly in here."

"The air conditioner, my dear," he said.

Sophia was in the living room. She sat quietly with her dogs to either side of her like two protective mini lions and her face showed defeat.

"We're leaving on the first flight to New York tomorrow," Sophia said in a small voice. "Donaldson's secretary made the arrangements."

"Today, you mean," Todd corrected her. "Look at the time. It's almost four a.m. We should probably just pack up and get to the airport early."

Sophia nodded. "I'm hoping by the time we get back the results of the autopsy will be ready."

"That fast?" I was incredulous. "I didn't think…"

"Well, not all the results," she said. "We'll have to wait for most of the toxicology reports. We will have preliminaries, you can be sure."

"I'll be on my way." Todd threw his head back as he drained the last drop in his glass.

"Me too." I pulled my shawl even closer and made to leave.

"Hold off a minute, I need to talk to you." Sophia motioned for me to stay.

I sat back down. One of the dogs jumped off the couch and stood in front of me yipping. I picked him up and rubbed his fur as he sat in my lap. He reminded me of my mother's dog who always wanted attention.

Sophia waited until Todd closed the door behind him and then she began to speak. "There's a lot you don't know. We need to talk about a few things."

I didn't want to interrupt. Whatever Sophia had to say, it had to be important. "We were having problems with them," Sophia said. "Doctor C. and Price were having a hard time… to put it delicately."

"I think I know…" His womanizing was common knowledge. I couldn't figure out why all the secrecy.

"No, actually, you don't," Sophia said. "You may be hearing this from the grapevine soon enough, although I really do hope that it doesn't come out. Doctor C. had called the police a few times. Price had some rather unorthodox behavior. As I said earlier, she tried to kill herself a couple of times. They might have been gestures. Probably were. She cut her wrists once and another time took an overdose of Vicodin tablets but then she changed her mind and told him. He called the police. Because of their positions at Windsor, she was transported to a city trauma hospital. They treated and released her immediately. The hospital administrator managed to keep it out of the news."

"Oh." What else was there to say? There had been no rumors about Dr. Price, only Dr. Campbell as far as I had been aware.

"Price told him she was pregnant before they were engaged."

I racked my brain. Had I been aware of a pregnancy? No. "There was no baby."

"Correct. She neither miscarried nor was ever pregnant. The fact that Doctor Campbell was known as a ladies' man didn't really help the situation. But she was an excellent surgeon with a thriving practice… hence, we kept them both on."

"That, I knew," I said. "I'm aware that he'd been involved with quite a few of us, I mean, the workers." I had to be careful. I didn't want a slip of the tongue to be my downfall.

"No one knows what ignited those two. But they were like dynamite sticks on conjoined wicks; always sizzling. We did everything to keep the fire down." Sophia shook her head. "He was quite a bit older than she... Doctor Price was lovely though... she was a beautiful woman."

"You're right, Sophia, but she looked so empty." I thought about the last time I saw her in the corridor. "A couple of days before we left on our trip I saw her at work. I thought it was strange that she didn't take any time off after his death."

"She said that she couldn't stand being in the house without him- that the house was very cold without his presence."

I attended a reception they had at the mansion before the wedding. The whole Operating Room staff had been invited. It was the loveliest home I'd ever set foot in. Marge's house, albeit warm and inviting, was no comparison to it. The decorators had done an incredible job with it... and now the inhabitants were dead. It was as though the house was some sort of a façade for others to marvel at while it hid the dark truth of the couple.

"I'm sure that it was awful for her going home to an empty house after work. It must have been a pretty dark place for her. Morning and night... I know all about that. Even though it was different, after Lou died, all I had was myself to face."

"And you did an admirable job of it. Now, I think it's time that you return to your room. We do need that little bit of sleep."

Sophia's words helped. As bullish as she could be, she had an incredibly sweet chord of kindness running through her.

I practically fell asleep before I hit the pillow.

Chapter 12

The pilot landed the Boeing gently on the J.F.K. runway. A few of the older passengers clapped when the plane successfully touched the ground. I knew that they were from la isla, because only islanders did that. The tiny gray haired man next to me crossed himself. No doubt they were relieved, and so was I, but how many of them were going back to a job where two of the most prominent surgeons were dead within a little more than a week of each other?

"Keep an eye on the clock, Daisy." Sophia was herself again, a battle ax ready to dive right back in. The dogs whined in their bags. They weren't happy about being treated like luggage. "Don't forget we're meeting at the office by two."

"No problem." I was resigned to whatever lay ahead and glad that I squeezed in a visit with my aunt and cousin before we had to jet back to New York again.

After disembarking we stopped to pick up our baggage. Even Sophia had given in and agreed it was easier to let the handler deal with the suitcases rather than try to stuff them in the overhead bins.

Todd was suddenly busy and unavailable making phone calls on his smart phone. It was easy to see how he kept people at bay with his prop. I could feel my phone vibrating in my pocket but couldn't figure out how to get the luggage, help care for the dogs, and answer it at the same time. It would have to wait. It was probably Letty who thought I was still in Puerto Rico. Maybe it was my father wondering how the visit with my aunt went. I continued to struggle with multitasking the luggage and the dogs when the phone buzzed in my pocket again. It would have to wait until later.

We went our separate ways when we reached the ground transportation. I helped Sophia into one cab, waved as she was driven off, and waited for the next cab. My hope for a quick resolution to the murder had turned into increased anxiety. From what I knew there hadn't been any arrests and with the killer free there were many questions that were still unanswered.

As I stood there waiting for a taxi to pull up I felt my phone vibrate again. Pulling it out of my pocket, I saw that I had missed three calls. The first was from my sponsor, Angela, who had returned my call. I thought that was nice of her because she was in the habit of not returning my calls.

The second call was from Allie and her voice sounded shrill on the message she left on my voice mail. "Doctor Price was found dead. We have to talk. As soon as you get this message, call me."

The nauseous feeling I was left with made me question myself. I couldn't ignore my intuition. Something about Allie's tone and message wasn't right. Maybe I shouldn't doubt my friend but there was something going on and before I put anymore trust into her I needed to find out what was creating that nagging feeling. I was eager to get home and pull a card on the situation- maybe I'd get some clarity.

Saving Allie's message, I moved on to the last and smiled once I heard the deep baritone voice of none other than Detective Rodriguez.

"Hi, it's me, Rod." I felt a sudden thrill go through my body that screamed yes, yes, yes! "I hear you're coming back sooner than planned. I'm hoping we can go out for a bite to eat. I'm also hoping I won't have to cancel at the last minute but at least you know what's been keeping me busy on the work front. Let me know if this works for you. I'll be around."

He was asking me out on a date. An actual date! That call was so pleasantly unexpected, it felt really good to receive it with all the craziness going around. If he didn't think it was a conflict of interest then I wouldn't worry about it either. Contrary to what I thought, Rod didn't laugh at my intuition and that felt really great. I was so excited to be asked on a date that his call would be the first I'd return. It seemed like forever since I'd been on one.

Going on a date with Rod could be so many things. Maybe he would want to check out the sights on the High Line or take in a movie. A club would be great but that would mean dancing and I wasn't ready for that yet. I could probably convince him that a quiet dinner was our best bet for a great date.

"Miss, Miss, please, you're holding up the line. You want the cab or not?" The dispatcher pulled me out of my head.

"Yes." I handed him my bag that he placed in the open trunk and told the cab driver where I was headed in Brooklyn.

Once settled in the taxi, I began drifting off for the remainder of the ride; I imagined how good it would be back in the apartment. I missed my bed after a couple of nights. Granted there was no private pool here, but my comfy place was like no other. It was mine and it was safe. The cab came to a stop in front of the brownstone. I paid the driver and waited for the receipt. I exited the back of the cab into the cool Brooklyn day. This business trip stuff was fabulous, all my expenses were reimbursed by Accounting, and I didn't have to pay for a thing.

It was a bit early but I had to stop in at Marge's. The last week had gone very fast and visiting Marge would ground me.

Fitting my key into the brass lock, I heard Jose's voice. "Is that you, jetsetter?"

"Yeah, I'm back." I pulled my bags in behind me. "If you'll help me, I'll give you my autograph."

Jose opened the door wide for me and took my larger bag. "What do you have in here? Bricks?" Putting it over to the side, he gave me a hug. "We missed you. You can claim the cat. She tried to go to bed with us. I told her that Rubio was allergic and she got offended."

"I'll be glad to take her." Ms. G. was already rubbing my legs with her body when I scooped her up. "Did those bad men hurt you?"

"Very funny, we didn't hurt her, just her feelings. Did you bring us pasteles?"

"No, I ate yours." I looked around. "Where are Marge and Rubio?"

"She's in her kitchen, where else would she be?" Jose said. "Rubio? I'm not sure."

"That doesn't sound too good."

"I'm sure he'll be home soon," Jose said. "Something about signing the lease for the gallery... there are studies that shows that wining and dining is good for business."

"I bet. I had a glass of scotch right under my nose... it was intense. I don't know how he does it."

"I think it becomes second nature like everything... practice." Jose picked my bags up to take them up to the fourth floor. "I'll bring these up for you and meet you down there in a minute."

"Great. I appreciate it," I said, cradling the cat as I walked down to Marge's kitchen. The tantalizing smell of something baking welcomed me.

"Hi, Marge, what is that?" I walked over to the

oven, about to open it.

"Leave it," Marge demanded. Ruffian opened one eye from his spot on the kitchen tile floor and promptly closed it. "Oatmeal and raisin cookies."

"When will they be ready?" I asked. "I'm starving."

"A new work group from the community board will be meeting here tomorrow. This batch is for them. The next batch will be for you."

"Okay, be like that." I sat down. "You have to hear this. Doctor Price, you know, Doctor Campbell's new wife, was found dead in their brownstone, just a couple of blocks away from here. They think it's a suicide."

"Wow, so what happened?" Jose's interest was keen as he walked through the door. "Suicide? How?"

"Well, they have to do an autopsy, they're not really sure yet. But pretty sure. It seems she had a history of trying."

"How terrible," Marge said. "A doctor... my goodness, one would think she'd get help for that."

"You would think that, wouldn't you? Apparently, she was a handful. He was no help either, having lots of affairs with people she crossed paths with every day. I can tell you this since you don't have any connection with the hospital. Sophia let me in on it. They had to call the police a few times for her. She cut her wrists, nothing deep but enough to leave scars. She even took an overdose of pills but told him as soon as she swallowed them. According to Sophia, she never did anything this bad before."

"His affairs must have been so trying for that poor woman," Marge observed.

"But if it was, why would she marry him anyway?" Jose asked. "She knew what kind of man he was. They worked together for quite a while before they married. Didn't you say they just got back from their honeymoon?"

I nodded. "Not that long ago. They just had the house redone too. It's all crazy. They lived with each other for some time before the wedding." I eyed the cookies as Marge took them out of the oven. "The other thing I didn't have a chance to tell you is that Allie might lose her job. They're saying she's responsible for the unit being unlocked. It's all weird. I'm not saying she's involved in this thing but there's something I can't put my finger on about her."

"I think you need to be wary of Allie," Marge agreed. "I realize she's your friend, but you have to listen to your intuition. Find out the truth, but don't get too close."

"I agree," Jose said. "It doesn't sound too kosher. Your friend could be dangerous."

"But I've known her for years," I said. "We worked that unit together all day." Still, I couldn't help but remember that she went into the locker room at the end of the day. Shaking my head, I reassured myself that she had no involvement in this. "She's a great nurse. I'm sorry, but I think the fact the door was left open is the security department's problem. Not hers. She had several patients she was tending to that afternoon. She was busy."

"Look, all we're suggesting is that you find out as much as you can. If she's as trusted a friend as you think, she'll tell you the truth."

"I'll talk to her. Marge, are you sure about those cookies?"

"I can see where your priorities are," Jose said. "If she gets one, I want one too."

Marge flicked her kitchen towel towards us. "You two are like big kids, go on, out!"

"Come on, Marge, please!" Jose pleaded with her but couldn't stop laughing at the site of her tiny frail body menacing us with a red and white checked towel.

"Okay, one each, but then I mean it… out!"

I grabbed a cookie and gave her a kiss on her soft cheek. She treated me like a grandmother and I loved her for it. "Thanks, Marge, I'm going, I'm going…" I couldn't help but smile on my way up the stairs.

After a few days away, going back into my apartment was like winning the Lotto. It was clear, clean, and all mine. It would be there for me tonight, but right now I needed to concentrate on getting to the office. There was so much going on.

※

Heads were going to roll unless Dr. Campbell's death was solved soon. Pushing my way past the media vans and stepping over cables were the easy parts of returning to the office. The looks of suspicion between staff members and whispers that stopped when I approached old friends in the corridor were harder to negotiate. I prepared a report of the presentation that Sophia would first have to okay before I delivered it to Mr. Donaldson. As I looked over the sheets in front of me, I heard a soft knock at the door.

"Come in." I could barely hide my annoyance. There was so much to get done and there had been one interruption after the other since I walked in. To top it off, Todd hadn't come in after all. He decided to take another day off and come in the next day. I had no idea of what he thought of himself but whatever it was, I didn't agree.

The door swung open and there was Rod, smiling sheepishly at me. "Couldn't wait to see you. I'm glad that you're back." He stood in my doorway looking all sorts of amazing.

I couldn't help but return the smile. "Uh, hi, I didn't

expect you here this afternoon. I mean, here, yes, as in the hospital here, but not in my office... you know what I mean." I felt myself blush. I'd give anything to get rid of that habit.

"Yes, I do." He nodded. "I thought I'd take a minute to say hello."

"Glad you did," I said. "I'm definitely looking forward to dinner with you."

"Great," he said. "Tonight?"

Being on the point of exhaustion I knew I should have said no. What was that I'd heard during my meetings? HALT. Don't let yourself get too hungry, angry, lonely, or tired. I was definitely tired and that usually got me closer to angry but if I had dinner I wouldn't be hungry...

"Daisy, are you in there?"

"Yes. I'm sorry. My thinking got a little carried away. How are things going here, in terms of the investigation?"

"We're kind of at a standstill." He turned away as he made the admission. "We've interviewed everyone and haven't come up with anyone yet. It's kind of embarrassing; we should have him by now."

"We'll have to talk about him. I don't think he's a he, I think he's a she." I stood up and folded my arms against my torso, ready for him to laugh.

"A she? Why do you think it's a she? Are you going for the nurse thing too?"

"Well, no, I don't really believe that any one of the nurses could do it," I said. "Or would do it, remember that dream thing I told you about the other night..."

Rod sighed. "And what about it?"

"Come on, hear me out," I said. "We talked about this already. I see things and I'm sharing it with you because I think it's going to be helpful, not because I want you to lose your job or anything."

"I don't doubt you but I need to have something a bit more substantial when I talk this out with my partner… you know, something other than 'this lady told me that she saw this in a dream'." Rod tilted his head to the door, indicating that Munroe was outside. "Gotta go, I'll text you later. Mexican okay with you?"

"Sounds great." I flashed him a smile and watched as the door closed behind him. Dinner tonight sounded like an excellent idea and I couldn't wait to see him again. I could practically hear another voice in my head warning me to go slow and take it easy where Rod was concerned.

"Daisy," Sophia called from the adjoining office. "Bring those reports in here. I'd like to look them over."

I jumped. "I'm sorry. I'll be right in."

"Bring them in and close my door behind you. We need to talk."

I bit my lip. The 'we need to talk' always rubbed me the wrong way. I walked into her office and closed the door behind me as she instructed. Before I could turn around she began lecturing me.

"I'm not really sure which is more inappropriate," Sophia said. "You flirting with the detective or, what I believe I heard you doing, giving psychic messages here. You're going to have to explain yourself. That is, if you can."

"I know I'm on thin ice… don't think I forgot that."

"Where do I hear an explanation in that?" Sophia's voice was razor sharp. "I kept you on and promoted you because I thought you'd be able to handle it. You're in a high profile position or maybe I should say that I am and you're my assistant. We are already in hot water and I am not going to let the hospital be jeopardized by your behavior."

"It's just that…" I tried to explain.

"Never mind." Sophia cut me off abruptly. "Don't say another word. Act as though I didn't hear or see you two together this afternoon. Let me believe that nothing is going on. I mean that. I want no evidence about what I thought I heard happen actually prove that I did. Get it? Now get back to work, before I change my mind."

Returning to my desk, I felt mixed emotions. I was grateful for the job but it felt awful having someone breathing down my neck. I thought if I were physically capable of walking on eggshells to appease Sophia it would be a neat trick. The real magic, however, would be to get to Allie before anyone else did. I had to know the truth of what was going on with my friend. I also needed to work through the conflict inside me that was mounting about her and she was the only one who could help me do that.

Chapter 13

"It's definite. I got my pink slip today." Allie brushed her hand listlessly on the arm of my couch. "I told you that they needed a fall guy, and that would be me."

I kept glancing at the clock. I wanted to connect with her but tonight was inconvenient. Rod was supposed to show up in an hour and I was anxious because I still had yet to get ready. What else could I do but open the door when she started ringing the doorbell? I leaned out the window to see who it was and there was Allie leaning against the stoop bannister. When I spoke to her through the intercom, I could tell by her sniffling that things hadn't turned out well. It amazed me that while I was Sophia's assistant, there was so many things I wasn't privy to.

"Do you want to stay here tonight?" I tried to figure out how to handle the situation. The clock arms seemed to be whirling around way too quickly. "We can talk more when I get back. I have a date… it's been a long time since I had one and I don't want to cancel it. Sorry."

"A date? When?" Allie pulled at my hem. "Who? When did you have time to meet someone?"

"It's Detective Rodriguez."

"Detective Rodriguez?" Her look of bewilderment tore at me. "You mean as in the guy that's investigating the murder? Daisy, how could you?"

"What's wrong with that? Really? He didn't arrest you, did he?"

"No, I guess you're right, I'm being silly," Allie agreed. "But no, I'm not taking you up on your offer. I've got an apartment and I should probably go home."

Just when I thought things were finally under control Allie burst into tears. I hurried to find the box of tissues that I knew were still hanging around from my early days of sobriety. Those days anyone could find me moping around and crying more than I thought possible. It was probably more of a detox from Lou than from the alcohol. At least that's what I told myself. Of course my sponsor, Angela, disagreed. There it was. The half-filled box of Kleenex was on the floor hidden to the side of the couch.

"Go later." I thrust a wad of tissues at her. Things were tough and I wanted to help her out in some way or another. "Right now, I want you here. We can talk when I get back. Just hang out for a while. Watch a movie. It's a good place. No one will bother you. I'm only going out to dinner. I'll be home early."

"He's a good looking guy," Allie said. "You might be out longer than you plan."

I shook my head. "That's not going to happen."

"Never say never."

"I'm going to take a quick shower and get ready to leave. Stay and we'll talk when I get back."

I stood up and Allie sunk into the cushions. It hadn't taken much to convince her. The street lamps were coming on and glowed through the windows.

"Okay," she said. "I'll wait. Do you mind if I get Chinese?"

"Be my guest," I said. I went into my bedroom and breathed a sigh of relief. I found a large clean towel and went into the bathroom. Mexican with Rod. I couldn't wait.

❊

The aroma of the stuffed enchilada wove its way into my nose. I cut into it and the cheese poured out onto the plate. I mixed it with a generous portion of frijoles and took a forkful.

"How is it that when something smells so good that

our mouths water?"

"We're just made like that." Rod laughed. "I heard it's those neurons. They're all connected."

"What do you know about neurons?" I adjusted the napkin in my lap. "Been around the hospital that long?"

"No, from my mom," he said and swallowed a bite of shredded beef while pouring more jalapeño sauce on his plate. "She's a nurse. She went to nursing school when I was in the eighth grade. I helped her study. I was lucky enough to memorize all the bones and muscles, just like her."

I was floored. Envisioning my own mother opening books and studying was something I just couldn't do. My mother was too busy cracking open the Johnny Walker Black. "Interesting. How about your dad?" I asked.

"He's a veteran of the force. He's a nurse, too."

"Get out. You're making this up."

"Haven't you heard about policemen who retire and go to nursing school?" he asked. "They take notes on their little pads. Seriously, my Pops works in the Emergency room at St. Mary's. My Mom is there, too, but she loves her some orthopedics."

I couldn't help but smile along with his amused expression. We waited while the server poured more water into our glasses. When Rod said he preferred to stick with water it was more than I could have ever asked for. The topic of alcohol didn't even come up. Rod pointed to the nacho bowl indicating a refill. The server bowed slightly and took it with him. Lila Downs swelled through the air, then Los Lonely Boys and, eventually, Los Tigres del Norte captivated us with their Mexican Norteño tunes.

"I'm really liking this." I blushed when I realized the words had actually come out of my mouth. "I don't think I was supposed to say that out loud."

"Well, I'm glad you did because 'I'm liking this,' too." He smiled at me with a black frijole set between two of his bright white upper teeth.

I dug into my bag for my cosmetic mirror. "Here, no offense."

We laughed as he excused himself to remove the offender. "That's what I like about you, no holds barred. You're not afraid to say anything, are you?"

"Oh, I don't know about that."

He seemed thoughtful. "You weren't afraid to tell me that you hear voices... spiritually, I mean."

"I'm still getting used to that myself. Now that you bring it up, I've been wondering whether the male and female figures in my dream were Doctor Campbell and Price. They're both dead now."

Rod raised his eyebrows. "They got the autopsy results today. They put a rush on it."

"And?" I grabbed on to the table. "Did she kill herself?"

"Stabbed. They found a puncture wound between intercostal six and seven."

"In the ribs! In her living room?" I asked. "With what?"

Rod scanned the room. All attention was fixed on a group at the bar slinging back tequila shots. The counter was lined up with tiny dishes of salt, lime, and several bottles of beer. Things were heating up and hard laughter filled the air.

"A dagger," he said. "There was a knife display on the wall. A collection of beautiful, very intricate designs. Not sure which one of them owned the collection but it was one of those knives that was used. The house was clean. No finger prints, no forced entry, no other weapons. No nada."

"Does that mean that she knew her murderer? Oh,

Rod." I held onto the edge of the table. "She must have let them in. She had to have known who it was."

"That could mean that anyone did it. From her mother to the postman."

"She was also bashed at her temple. One of the first responders found a heavy statue at her side. No prints on it either."

"You never really thought that she killed Doctor C. Did you?"

"The spouse is usually the first suspect," he said as he ladled a bit of shredded beef and rice onto a piece of soft taco. "You know that. Haven't you watched any crime shows?" He didn't wait for me to answer. "The cleaning lady was there earlier that day. There wasn't a fingerprint throughout the whole house. It seemed almost sterile. I know they were surgeons but it was pretty ridiculous."

"So little that we really know about people."

"By the way, keep this quiet. We're not saying anything about the weapon. That bit of information won't be in the news. We're hoping that while questioning, the murderer will give themselves away if they bring up this fact. We're also waiting for the toxicology tests to come through."

"You won't hear anything from me about that. I have to ask you something and I hope you'll answer this one." I put my fork down next to my plate. "My friend, Allie, is she a suspect?"

He continued to dig through the mound of rice and beans on his plate. "Why? Do you think she should be one?"

"You're good. I like how you just did that. Answered my question with another question... she got fired today." I sighed. "They blame the fact that all the doors to the O.R. suite were not locked on her watch."

"Fall guy," he said, "or I should say girl. That's a security issue, not Nursing. I can tell you that much."

"She's at my house. Came over this evening, she was beside herself- frantic. You know that we were together that day. But I think there's more she knows that she's not telling us."

"Like what?"

"Well, I have this feeling that she's holding on to some information. I'm not sure what it could be, but she is."

"Think more, or look more closely, what do you see?"

What a thrill! Here I was being encouraged to look for more information by the detective on the case. I closed my eyes and, in my mind's eye, I was back on the beach in Puerto Rico. Images played in front of my third eye. Water. The surf was rough. I pulled my mind back into the restaurant.

"She was emotionally connected to him. I see water. Water is of the emotions. She wasn't happy about whatever it was."

"Was she close to Doctor Campbell?" Rodriguez seemed thoughtful. "I'm trying to remember the interview I had with her after the first murder. She didn't let on if she was."

"Allie was upset that one of the nurses was going to charge him with sexual harassment."

"What are you talking about? As far as I can tell he easily got whatever he wanted. This is the first that I'm hearing about this."

"Not according to Miss Taylor, one of the supervisors. She hated him. Or I should say the way he used his power to get whatever he wanted."

"That's it? Your knowing that he was about to face

a sexual harassment charge doesn't equal to two murders."

"But what if there's more? There could be you know."

"I'm a little curious," Rod said. "How well do you know your friend?"

"We worked together for quite a while before I transferred to work with Sophia."

"What else? Did you two go out? Shopping? Drinks?" he asked. "I'm wondering if there is more to her than you even know. Working with someone doesn't mean that you're bosom buddies, know what I mean?"

"Yeah, I know… we basically saw each other at work," I answered. "It's not like we went on vacation together or hung out at each other's houses. I did find it strange to have her pop up at my place today. She might have come over for drinks a long time ago but not recently, that much I know."

"That answers that. You don't really know her, do you?"

I shrugged. "Would I swear on a stack of Bibles for her? No, if that's what you mean. But what I've really been thinking about is why did the first Mrs. Campbell divorce him?"

"Probably because of his extracurricular activities."

"He was a little whack, I know, I dated him for a little while."

Rod's color perceptibly changed. "How does that compute here? This is the second time you're telling me this. Because if there's not a good reason to talk about it, let's not."

"Don't be silly," I said. "It's important to what we're talking about, but if you're jealous, forget it; I'll talk to Detective Munroe instead."

Rod's body sagged in his chair. "Okay, you got me.

I'm being ridiculous. I almost turned thirteen there. I know that I'm not your first boyfriend."

"Boyfriend? What? Are you my boyfriend is the first question?" I shifted in my seat. This was going way too fast for me. "I don't think so. This is our first date."

"Can't we count dinner with Mike and Letty?" he asked slyly.

"No, a movie, at least a movie… maybe a walk on the boardwalk or something, but not dinner at Mike and Letty's, that doesn't count as a date."

"Okay, gotcha." Rod brightened up a bit. "So what were you gonna tell me about him being a whacko."

"He had a weird schedule. He said he'd get up at three in the morning to run." I felt better once I got that out. No need to share about the couple of nights I woke up to find that empty indent on the sheets where he had been all too briefly.

"Intense, I'd say, why would he do that?" Rod mused about the added facts.

"He was a compulsive type of guy. It's like he couldn't help himself. He was so controlled with everything else, as a surgeon. If there was something he felt he needed to do, he did it. Like having a snack attack. He'd get this urgency and become possessed."

"A snack attack?" Rod laughed. "I like your description."

"When I get home, I'm going to ask Allie what her big secret is. I'll get it out of her."

"Now, let's forget about this case and let's talk about us. That's what a date is for, agreed?"

"Agreed."

We chatted through the rest of the meal about our not too similar childhoods and eventually looked over the dessert menu, finally ordering a double order of flan con queso. I didn't want the evening to be over.

✻

By the stillness in the apartment I could tell that Allie was gone. A soft rap at the door pulled me away from my thoughts back to the living room.

"Yes?" I opened it a crack to see Jose standing in the hallway. "Come in, hurry. Did you see my friend Allie? Did you see when she left?"

"If you read the shells for your friend, it would show irosun." He stood in the doorway with his arms crossed.

"What? My friend, I asked, did you see my friend?"

"Irosun. It means 'no one knows what's at the bottom of the sea.' The Oddu shows four mouths open. It's how the Orisha speak. There's a lot more to your friend than you think you know."

"Yeah, well, I could have told you that without throwing shells. I got the image of her and water. Whatever it is, it's deep I'd say and I hope she doesn't drown. Can the shells tell us where in the world Allie is and why she's mixed up in this? Can they tell us who the murderer is?"

"Where's your reverence, Daisy?"

"I'll search for it in the bedroom while I'm looking to see if she left a note or something in there."

I walked into my bedroom while Jose went into the kitchen with a promise to make lemonade.

"Hey, I got what you're looking for!" he yelled. "Out here! She left a note. She taped it to the shelf in the fridge."

Jose stood in front of the refrigerator and read aloud.

I know that you are probably mad. I would be too.

Forget about looking for me. You won't find me. I didn't do it.
You've been good to me, too good.
    Thanks, Allie

    There were crumbs in the sink, along with a frying pan that had gummy cheese covering the inside. She must have changed her mind about the Chinese food and helped herself to a grill cheese sandwich. The bowl on the counter that had held a couple of stark crimson pears was empty. Wherever she went, Allie had made sure that she wasn't going to be hungry. I went into the bathroom for my cosmetics case. I got the tweezers out and returned to the kitchen. Finding a clean sandwich baggie, I picked up the note with the tweezers and slipped it inside. Contrary to what Rod thought, I spent plenty of evenings in front of the television watching NCIS. I'd show the note to him and Munroe in the morning. Now, all I wanted was a good night's sleep.

    "No offense, Jose, I'd really love to chat with you but I do have to get some sleep. The reality is I flew in from P.R. this morning and haven't stopped since the plane landed."

    "No problem. We'll talk tomorrow. I wanted to update you on my honey."

    "Never mind, tell me now."

    "I think he's got someone new in his life."

    "Are you for real?"

    "That's not the worse. I think it's a woman."

    "Oh, Jose. No! He'd never do that."

    "Money talks… the owner of the building where the gallery is in is a woman. Selena Montoya. She's gorgeous but dangerous. I don't know this for sure but I feel it. Something is happening, I know Rubio for way too long to not know when he's hiding something."

"Well, it's up to you to ask him. You have to find out. Remember the slogan 'think, think, think.' Don't let your overthinking get the best of you."

"Yeah, whatever."

"Hey, when was the last time you went to a meeting?"

"I'm not sure."

"I was able to get to one in Puerto Rico. How about we meet early in the morning? We could both use one. My thinking is getting screwy too."

Jose agreed. "Yeah, you're probably right. I'm so paranoid right now. I don't know if it's the fact that I'm not working. I'm used to bringing home the bucks. Real bucks. This business of having to depend on what Rubio brings home isn't working either. He's an artist. If he happens to sell a piece it's great, but sometimes it can be pretty dry in that department."

"That's your problem. I bet he's not doing anything wrong. Why would he be with Selena Montoya or whatever her name is? He's not an idiot. Rubio's just doing business. Just because he's an artist doesn't mean he isn't a businessman. A person can do both."

"I hope so." He seemed so gloomy.

"Trust in it. I believe it."

Chapter 14

We met in the conference room that somehow became the police interrogation room at the hospital. Liz Munroe studied her blood red nail tips as she began to speak. "She went on a trip. That doesn't make her a criminal. We didn't ask her to stay in town... did we?"

I paced. "She just lost her job..."

Munroe's right eyebrow peaked up. "And?"

"The point is," Rod argued, "that we're in the middle of an investigation and this lady takes off. She was the last one working on the unit the evening of the murder."

"Can you explain to me who you mean when you say 'we'?" Munroe stifled a yawn. "The day I got this assignment there were only the two of us."

Thank goodness I started out the day at a meeting with Jose. Although the overriding message about using 'restraint in pen and tongue' was my favorite one, taking a deep breath and staying on pause for a minute was proving to be difficult around Munroe. I decided to ignore her comment and try again.

"Allie was at my house last night and I brought you the note that proves she's missing..."

"Should I correct that for you or would you like Detective Rodriguez to have the honor?" Munroe hissed at me. "Missing means that she disappeared. The note, written by her hand, according to you, says she's leaving. How can I put this? She's not missing. She's left by her own accord. Don't you get it?"

"Oooh!" I held my head in my hands. "Why is it...?"

Rod stepped in between us. "Stop it you two, this isn't helping. Okay, Allie wasn't a suspect but lost her job because of a lack of judgment according to her boss. The two of you were the last on the unit that day."

"No, wait a minute." I looked up at him. "I do get it, Detective. But this is what I don't get… we weren't the last two there, there was an evening shift because of the overflow of late surgeries. The patients weren't transferred to the surgical unit after all because they were short staffed. We had an evening nurse, Miss Ford…"

"Yes, yes, we've been all over this." Munroe cut me off. "I take it that you didn't tell her that Miss Ford was cleared. For goodness sake, she's been a nurse here for thirty years."

"No, not Miss Ford, there were a few patients still there." They looked at me like I was a mad woman. I could see that they weren't buying any of my speculations. "Don't you see? It had to be one of the clients."

"A post-operative client?" Munroe scoffed. "Excuse me, but I have some real work to do. Rodriguez?" She looked at her partner expectantly.

"I'll be there in a few," he said. "Wait for me."

Munroe slithered out of the room closing the door quietly behind her. I felt a wave of tension leave the room with her and sighed. Rod and I stood face to face. Last night seemed so long ago, as if it were a different time and place. At this moment, it was like we were quite possibly two different people.

"What makes you think it was one of the patients?" he asked. "They were unconscious, weren't they?"

"Of course not." This was becoming more than irritating. Taking time to wake up from anesthesia didn't mean that they were unconscious. "Don't either one of you think anyone else has a worthy thought in their head?"

"Detective Munroe is my partner and she's waiting for me outside. I really don't want to go into this but I do want to hear your theory."

"The patients in the recovery room have been under anesthesia but most of it is local. They're awake pretty soon after surgery. Groggy, yes, but they can still function. None of them were having major surgery."

"Then why are they still in the recovery room?" he asked. "They're supposed to be going home on the same day, right?"

"It's not always that simple." I did my best to explain. "Sometimes they have to stay to be monitored if they have a reaction to the anesthesia, or they might have a surgical drain that needs to be watched... believe me, the doctors try to get them out as soon as possible but if someone's blood pressure is too high or low they need to stay in for observation. Plastic surgeries, though optional, can be deadly. I've seen it happen."

"You have?" Rod looked at me with renewed respect.

"Your mother's a nurse. Don't you know this stuff already?"

"Well, she doesn't share the details with me. Please go ahead."

"I'm not that close to the clients ever, but I do have to be on the alert to call the codes, make sure that the blood results get back fast, you know, all the background stuff no one ever really thinks about."

"Look, I think this is going to take longer than I have just about now." Rod was apologetic. "I'll be back in the afternoon. Can you print a list of the clients that were here that day?"

"Sure, but don't waste your time on the list of men you'll see on that list." I was feeling more and more confident about my theory. "It was a woman and that is one detail that I'm sure of."

"Please, Daisy, just get the list. See you in a bit."

⚜

Sophia walked into my office pushing a metal cart filled with files. "I want to look through these with you."

"Of course, what's up?"

I wondered what new project she was cooking up now. We were busy enough as it was. Sophia was great for bringing up new ideas and then having me translate them into completed surveys, reports, and anything else that would bring productivity to the work place. We were only now getting over the presentation on recidivism we were so busy with in Puerto Rico. With the murder investigation, however, everything else had fallen by the wayside.

"These are files on the cases that were seen the last day that Doctor Campbell did surgery before he was murdered. Daisy, you are in my utmost confidence on this. I expect that you will not discuss any of these cases with your new friend, Detective Rodriguez. Agreed?"

"I'd like to agree but he just asked me to print out a list of all the clients who had surgery that day," I said softly.

"I see." She paused and glanced at the files before looking back at me. "I'd still like to look at the charts before we turn them over to the detectives. Sit with me. I'll need you to take some notes."

I convinced myself that there really wasn't a conflict of interest. That I was simply doing what my boss wanted and she was cooperating with the police. All I had to do was concentrate on doing the next right thing.

"No problem. I understand."

"I was sure you would," Sophia said. "We've already discussed how the hospital can't afford the bad publicity. The newspapers and reporters are like dogs with bones. They should be reporting on more noteworthy things." Her annoyance was palpable. "It might have naturally taken a back seat but that all changed when Doctor Price was killed right in their home. A general sense of safety is gone... home, work. Those are places we usually feel safest..." She took a deep breath, sifted through the files and handed them over to me. "We need to find out who that murderer is. The detectives have been quite busy, I'm sure, but things are not moving quickly enough for us here in our small community. This is supposed to be a healing community. I've said my piece. Now, let's get started."

There were a dozen charts. Two of them were for male clients. That left ten files to peruse.

"Sophia, I know you hate it..."

"Just go ahead, tell me what you need to, no preambles please." Sophia scrutinized me over her reading glasses.

"First of all, I think we need to focus on women. Secondly, we should probably focus on women that were in Doctor Campbell's age group." I hesitated for a second. "These are just some thoughts I have. Well, it's more like a feeling than actual thoughts."

"Very well, I do commend you on your use of intuition. I just hesitate when it comes to the police or the public." She looked at me for a moment. "You realize that one can be arrested in New York City for fortune telling, don't you?" I could feel her gaze burn into me. "I've spent a lifetime listening to my intuitive side, although most people wouldn't think I give my hunches a second thought. That's how I've come so far in my business life. If it feels right, then I follow it. This feels right. Let's start looking," she said before she opened the first chart.

Sophia had this way of always surprising me by

saying something nice when I least expected it. I never expected her to tell me that she also honored her intuitions. Two amazing and surprising admissions and I loved them both.

We each took a chart and began to sift through the possibilities. The front sheets in the folders held the intake information for each of the clients. These showed the demographics, reasons why they were being admitted, and what the client thought was his or her problem.

"Mrs. Moore," I read aloud from the first chart I opened. "Sixty-seven years old. Admitted for dissection of a mole that she noticed was changing color on her left shoulder. That wouldn't be plastic surgery, would it?"

"Interestingly enough, sometimes the surgeons use Sixth Saturday for an overflow of the cases that they're unable to get to during the week." Sophia knew the system well. "Sixth Saturday is a money maker. The hospital will never say no to that."

"Does she stay on the list?" I flipped through a couple of the other folders "I say that we stick to women from the age of twenty-one to sixty. No offense, but I don't think that Doctor C. would have a personal connection with any women outside of that range."

"Sounds like a good idea."

I continued onto the next chart. "Josephine Davis. Thirty-five. Bilateral breast reconstruction. She had a double mastectomy ten years ago. My goodness, she was just a child. Twenty-five. This is a possibility; long surgery. She should have been done during the week, too. Let's put this one on the stack of possibilities."

"She would probably have been too out of it post-surgery to be involved in a murder." I opened and read from the next chart. "Joanne Richards. Forty-two. Repair of deviated nasal septum. Translation: nose job. A definite yes." I placed it to the side making a new pile.

"Margery Goldstein." Sophia scanned the front page. "No, not this one."

"No, Sophia, you have to read it out loud," I protested. "We're in on this together."

"This is disturbing. Another deviated septum. A fifteen-year-old." Sophia shook her head. "The child hasn't stopped growing yet. Her face will catch up to the size of her nose if she would be a little patient."

"What about this one, sounds like a keeper," I read. "Allison Montes. Fifty-four-year-old. Excision of multiple skin lesions and resection of abdominal flap. A tummy tuck to you and me."

"That would be a keeper," Sophia agreed. "Here's a thirty-one-year-old who came in for removal of bilateral breast prostheses. Actually, it says she wanted to go from bra size 36 DD to 34C. A bit of a nip and tuck, I'd say. Her original surgery was at age 18. Maturity caught up both emotionally and mentally. My goodness! The things we do with adolescent yearnings."

"We all do things that we might regret when we're a bit older and, hopefully, a little wiser."

"Cliché, but true. I'm not here to judge, just pick out possible suspects. Oh, her name is June Daniels."

"Have you thought of what we're going to do with the list that we pick out, once we have it?" I was getting restless. "We're going to have to be careful with this."

"Would you please stop tapping with that pen?" I hadn't noticed what I was doing before Sophia barked at me. "Thanks, dear. We need to wear kid gloves or in our case, surgical gloves. I'm not exactly sure what our next steps will be but this is our focus for today. Let's move forward, Daisy. I have to get these back to Medical Records."

"How did you get them?"

"Easy enough, but let's not lose our focus."

To have yet another person telling me not to lose focus was annoying, but I was starting to get used to all of the people around me saying the same thing, all the time.

"JaneMarie Fiorello," I read aloud. "Not Jane Marie but JaneMarie. Funny… she's a big possibility. Forty-five. Admitted for an under eye job. Removal of excess baggage there and around her tush."

"Please keep the professionalism in this, Daisy." Sophia snapped at me. "No need to disrespect the clients."

"I'm just reading what it says here. A medical student wrote this one up. If you don't believe me, look for yourself." The phone rang as I handed the chart over. "Should I get that?"

"Yes, of course." Sophia sat back in her chair.

I reached over and answered my desk phone. The open door policies both in phone calling and walk in visits to the administrator were handled with precision. It was important to have everyone think that a policy actually existed when in fact it didn't. I was becoming skilled at keeping people at bay and the result was that they were left feeling as though they received excellent service although they had never actually spoken to the administrator.

'It's Mrs. Campbell.' I wrote with a felt tip pen on a post it and held it out for Sophia to read.

Sophia shook her head vehemently from side to side while mouthing the word 'no.'

Without missing a beat, I responded to Mrs. Campbell. "She's not here right now. If you'd like, I can leave a message for her to call you as soon as she returns."

I listened to Mrs. Campbell as she shared the news that her young son, Ted, was missing. Sophia and the Campbell family went way back.

"This is serious, Sophia. Mrs. Campbell was distraught. It seems that Ted is missing. She thinks he's run away."

Sophia groaned and covered her eyes with her hand. "Daisy, would you please make a nice hot pot of coffee, dear? Please?"

"Sure." I stood up but Sophia put a hand up to stop me.

"Never mind that," she said. "We have to be quick. I must return her call but first let's finish looking at the charts. We have to complete this as soon as possible. Before we know it we'll be looking at a law suit and the courts will subpoena the charts."

"Is that really possible? What grounds would there be for a law suit?"

"Believe me, someone will find something," Sophia responded. "This country is fertile ground for lawsuits. You do know that anyone can sue for anything. As long as they find a lawyer to take the case it's possible. Right now, I'm hoping that it will be the state against the found murderer or murderers as the case may be."

"Gotcha... but look at this, here's another chart. Maggie Bartholomew. Twenty-eight years old." I squinted and tried to make out the handwriting. "She came in for, let's see, a, wouldn't you know it, another rhinoplasty."

"These nasal reconstructions are definitely the most sought out surgeries, aren't they? I say, yes, put her on the possible stack."

"Okay, next." My mind zeroed in on the next two. "I remember Allie and I spoke about these two. It wasn't the first time that these clients were here for cosmetic surgery."

"I daresay that some people become quite addicted to improving their appearances."

"Here goes, the first was Garden Stills, fifty-eight years old." I continued to read. "She came in for a neck reconstruction."

"Add her onto the yes pile." Sophia sounded weary and it was only ten o'clock in the morning. We had a full day ahead.

"The last chart here, females only, belongs to Mrs. Antoinette Jacques."

"Mrs. Dr. Jacques?" Sophia asked.

"Dr. Jacques, you mean as in radiologist Dr. Jacques?"

"Yes, look at the address. They have a house in the Hamptons but I think their city address is in Chelsea."

"Yes, the address is right on West 12th Street." I opened the chart to show Sophia. "The West Village?"

"I guess you're right."

I knew those neighborhoods well. There were great meetings at Perry Street in the Village and also a Ninth Avenue meeting in Chelsea. I went to that one by accident. Unlike the few I'd gone to before, that one was strictly a men's meeting. They were welcoming but I knew that I should try to find a women's or a mixed one, there were plenty of those. Besides, since I lived in Brooklyn, it was too far for me to go on a regular basis. They did, however, save my rear end on quite a few days that were filled with boredom and the desire to have a piña colada, or maybe six of them, was overwhelming.

"What surgery did she have planned for that day?" Sophia kept me on track.

"Another neck reconstruction."

"Last year she had her eye area smoothed out and breasts lifted," Sophia volunteered. "I remember how well she looked at their family holiday party. She admitted to me that it was the surgery that helped her have a new outlook on life."

"Outlook on life?" I placed that folder on top of the others. "It's interesting how surgery can do that for some people. I should try it. The therapy and meetings have helped me to change mine. Things can be a drag at times, not that I'm complaining."

"You're also about twenty years younger than Mrs. Jacques." Sophia was thoughtful in her response. "Things change my dear. Feeling good on the outside can really lift one's spirits."

"Along with one's breasts, I guess." I sighed. "I don't mean that in a bad way. I just never thought about it before. When I was growing up, cosmetic surgery was never on the radar for the women I knew. You dealt with what you got. Only rich people had the money to consider it. My mom and aunts were happy to have food on the table and clothes on their backs."

"You've come a long way." Sophia smiled. "Just think, one day you might be on the table for a neck lift or varicose stripping. Now, hand me those last two charts, there might be something here that we need to look at."

As I handed her the charts, I had a flash of something but I couldn't put my finger on it. Not just yet. "What are we going to do with this information?"

"First, dial up Mrs. Campbell for me; I need to return the call."

As Sophia spoke on the phone, I pulled the last two charts apart to make copies of the most pertinent information. I convinced myself that no one would find out that I did this. Once Sophia returned the charts we'd lose the opportunity to retrieve any information. Being aware of how easy it was to know who made database searches convinced me that looking on the computer was not how we wanted to go about unraveling information. I wanted to cover our tracks, making sure that nothing came back to us.

Sophia hung up. Before she spoke she rubbed at her eyes with her index finger and thumb. I could see the stress in her face.

"Just as you said, Ted disappeared," Sophia said. "He's extremely upset about his father's death, which was expected since they were very close." Sophia nodded in approval when she noticed that I made the copies. "Their other son, Charles, hasn't been in contact with his mother at all since he attended the family service. He returned to Baltimore immediately. That must mean he hasn't been much of a support for his younger brother." She reached out for me to hand her over the papers I just copied and placed them inside a folder. "He's a researcher and a surgeon. He was never that close to his parents. He was very shy as a child and very independent as well. The only thing that lit a spark in his eye was chemistry and medical school." Sophia paused for a moment as if trying to imagine Charles in an intimate setting was something impossible to do. "He's probably sharing his emotions with his fiancée. Apparently, he's about to be married."

"I saw Ted with Mrs. Campbell right after the memorial service. He was so upset. He's just a kid."

"Yes, he is," Sophia answered. "She asked that we keep an eye out for him. He practically grew up here. Now, let's figure out how we'll pursue more information on these clients."

Chapter 15

I stood at the copier making an extra set of the documents we decided might give us some clues. If I meditated at home with them near I might get even more details, but first I had to deal with the paper jam in the first drawer of the printer. The machine made my life miserable at times and this was one of them. I wished I could take it out back and blast it with a baseball bat.

As I tried to figure out where the paper jam was coming from, I felt my phone buzzing at my waist.

"Yes." I cradled the phone between my neck and shoulder.

"It's me."

"Allie, where are you?" I was relieved to hear her voice but also a bit angry. There was a little too much drama where she was concerned. I couldn't help but be sarcastic. "Did you run out of cheese sandwiches?"

"I'm sorry about that. I needed to get away. But I decided it's better to face up to everything. We need to talk."

"You had your opportunity." I gave the copier drawer one big shove and crossed my fingers. The colossal machine was way too sensitive for its size. "What the heck is wrong with you? Disappearing like that? I was worried when you weren't there when I got home."

"Can I come over again, tonight?"

"Okay, but really, no theatrics, okay? This is serious stuff."

"I'll be there about seven."

I felt a twinge of discomfort about having Allie over. Maybe I should have Rod there too, I thought. Yes, I would ask him to come over when he came to pick up the confounded list and wondered whether he'd actually need it once we heard what Allie had to say.

❊

Allie resembled a corpse bride. Her face was pale and it looked like she hadn't slept in a week although it had only been a couple of nights seen I'd last laid eyes on her.

"This could be a party except for the fact that it's not." I placed a tray of cookies that I picked up at Regina Bakery on my coffee table in front of all three of them. "These are good but I wish they'd put more fruity goo in the middle. Help yourselves."

"I guess I should start since we're meeting because of me." Allie turned to Jose. "We haven't been formally introduced. I'm Allie."

"I'm Jose," he said. "It's good to meet you."

I was glad that glad that neither Rod nor Allie looked at him strangely. He was dressed in his whites and he told me that he never knew what to expect when it came to people's reactions of his attire. Even though it sounded shallow, I was incredibly attracted to his spiritual life but I wasn't sure if I could deal with wearing white for a year. It seemed too complicated when all I really felt for was a simple spiritual life, something that I could wear internally, and not have to experience everyone gawking over me or judging me because of my outfits.

"So, you called me, why'd you disappear?" I wasn't in the mood to pussyfoot. Two murders were serious business and I didn't trust Allie like I did before this had all started.

"It's a bit embarrassing here, to say this in front of everyone, especially because I don't really know you two." Allie closed her eyes and sat back on the couch. "The truth is I'm pregnant."

"What!" I hadn't been prepared for this news. "Pregnant?"

"Yes, Doctor Campbell." Allie turned beet red. "Price knew. Suffice it to say they were not happy about it. I told him before the wedding. He ignored me. Said it was impossible. So, I got angry and told Price. She laughed, Daisy, she laughed right in my face." Her voice deepened with anger.

"Oh, Allie, that must have been terrible," I said. Suddenly the vision of Dr. Campbell speaking with a nurse in the recovery room area was crystal clear. "It was you who spoke with Doctor C. right before we left that evening, wasn't it?"

"I did stop to talk with him but he was very much alive when I left to meet up with you." Tears started streaming down Allie's face. "He told me that he'd be very happy if he never set eyes on me again."

I couldn't help but hug her. Her whole demeanor pulled at my heart strings. I let her go and got up to put the kettle on the stove. A little tea would calm Allie. It always helped me when I was upset. As I walked into the kitchen, the idea that I seemed to be turning more like Marge made me smile. While filling the kettle with water, I gave a silent prayer of thanks that I hadn't gotten pregnant from that man. I shivered when I thought of how dangerous the whole thing actually was.

Waiting for the water to boil, I watched from the kitchen as the two men sat quietly, allowing Allie a few minutes to gather her emotions.

"I never thought the first time I'd share news like this that it would be under these circumstances," she said.

I walked back into the living room. "No wonder you acted so strangely," I said. "But the remaining issue is that two people are dead. Who did it is a question that still needs to be answered."

"What about that woman that you said came to see him that night?" Allie's voice was full of hope. "If we can find her maybe then we can find out who the murderer is."

I addressed Jose. "I was kidding before when I asked you if the shells could tell you who the murderer was, but do you think it's at all possible?"

He placed his hand out in front of his chest. "I don't know about that. I guess anything is possible but I'm not the person to do that kind of thing. I'm a iyawó. Brand new, remember?"

The kettle whistled and I went into the kitchen and poured the boiling water in a porcelain teapot and placed teacups around it on a tray. Placing it on the table next to the three, I realized we were all looking at each other. I broke the silence with my next question. "Could we have a misa on this? I spoke with Hector. He said I'm ready."

"Misa?" Allie asked. "What's that?"

"A spiritual séance," I explained.

"Well, I'm not really sure," Rod said. "It's not in the detective how to handbook."

"I say call him," Jose suggested. "Padrino knows what we can and can't do."

I raised my eyebrows. "What am I saying? I don't think I'm ready to do this." I went into the kitchen with the excuse of getting something else to snack on. I came back out with a tin of shortbread cookies and placed them next to Allie. "Here guys, sugar is right there. If you need milk, let me know."

"Can I be at the séance?" Allie asked. "I'm a little curio…"

"No, I don't think so." Jose cut her off. "Sorry, Allie, I know we just met and all but I don't think you should be there."

Allie blanched. "What gives you the right to make this type of decision? We're all here because of me. Anyway, just give me one good reason why I shouldn't be part of the telepathy thing."

"You're pregnant. It'll be the first time we do this as a group. I just think it's better without you there. No offense." He raised his palms toward her.

"Yeah, I kind of agree too," Rod said. They all looked at me. "Daisy?"

"Agreed." I put my cup down on the coaster. "Sorry, Allie, but you really haven't been involved in this sort of stuff. The whole thing is really close to you too, being that you were in so much conflict around Doctor Campbell and Price. I wouldn't want any trouble around you, not that I expect any… I just want to be careful, that's all."

"When do you think you can do this? Can it be done tomorrow?" Allie asked. "I would really like it if we got as much information as soon as possible. I don't know much about this thing but I think I'd feel better having more information on Arthur. I'm in the early stages of my pregnancy and I don't want to be so upset all the time. That's how my pregnancy started and I don't think it would be good for my baby to be born in that kind of environment."

"For what this is worth, Allie," Jose addressed her directly. "I wouldn't want you to be dependent on the outcomes of this. Maybe you should find another way to de-stress. Maybe you can try meditating."

Rod stood up and stretched to ease the increasing tension in the room. "I've got an early morning ahead. You guys let me know what's good for you and I'll tell you if I can make it."

Jose nodded. "Well, I'm good just about for any

time. I'm not working right now. You guys let me know, but the sooner the better."

"I can do evenings. I already know that my weekend calendar is empty," I admitted. "I'll give Hector a call. I'm actually late in setting something up with him."

"I'll butt out," Allie said. "I promise, but you have to let me know all the details."

"Don't worry. Just don't disappear again. We're a motley crew to begin with so let's do it right. I'll keep you in the loop. I'm hoping that he's going to be available for this weekend. It's a long shot but anything is possible."

※

The sun was setting and the natural lighting had turned into an orangey glow. There were still no curtains blocking the windows but my living room was beginning to dim. It had been a few days since we met with Allie and now Hector, Rod, Jose, and Ana sat around the coffee table. The light was perfect for the events that were about to begin.

The coffee table had been covered with a white cloth. On it was a large clear bowl of water, a couple of vases filled with white flowers, and two lit candles. The table at the side of the couch held bottles of cologne, a prayer book, cigars, matches, and a few other items. There was a bottle of rum, a large clean coconut shell, that Jose called a jicara when he lent it to me for the evening, and a large bouquet of rhododendron leaves that he called 'lucky leaves.' He explained that the spirits sometimes wanted a drink of rum but I shouldn't worry about having to drink it. He explained that he never had to when he participated in a misa.

"What else would you like to ask before we start?" Hector gave us another opportunity to ask questions.

"Jose's done this with me quite a few times and Daisy once, correct? That means you know everything you have to know." He smiled at us.

Jose leaned back on the cushioned sofa. "Are you sure that it's okay for me to be here, Padrino?"

"As long as I'm here to watch over you," Hector said. "I wouldn't want you doing this without me." He turned to me. "This misa is for you. There has to be a focus."

"What if…?" I began.

Hector interrupted me. "If we get any information on the goings on related to the business at your work, I won't mind. But we aren't going out of our way trying to get names of murderers. That might prove too dangerous."

"Okay, I guess I would like the focus to be where I need to be in my spiritual life." There, I said it in front of everyone one.

"I'd like you to sit in this chair." Hector pointed to a chair that he removed from the kitchen. Underneath it he placed a medium sized glass of water. He wiped the chair down with a white cloth and threw red rose petals on it. I knew he did something to the glass but his back was turned to me so I couldn't see what that was.

Ana smudged the group with sage and frankincense. I was a bit nervous with her in my living room. Ana was well-known for her spiritual abilities. She owned a botánica in Park Slope for years and as much as I had wanted to peek in I never did have the nerve. Ana was very quiet and reassuring. She apparently separated her ego and attitude from her legendary psychic skills and acted like a normal person. I was grateful for this. Jose told me that ego was a big problem for some people and he had to separate 'principles from personalities' when he chose to follow this spiritual path.

I met Ana at the first misa I attended with Jose, she was his ayubona. Jose explained that being an ayubona was sort of being like a second godparent, a spiritual guide to him. Although, they were well respected elders in the Orisha traditions, both Hector and Ana were also very talented spiritualists. I still wasn't really sure what exactly the differences were because I was still new to these spiritual practices but I knew one focused on the ancestral spiritual world and the other on the paths of the Orisha.

"We might as well begin," Hector said. "Can someone turn the music off? I'd like it quiet here." He opened a thin paperback book with an orange and yellow cover and began to read to us.

I took a deep breath. I'd forgotten about the prayers that were read at the beginning of the misa. No wonder it was called a Mass, just different than the type I went to on Sundays as a child. As I closed my eyes I could feel my anxiety begin to creep up and I decided to focus on Hector's voice. I took a deep breath and became relaxed as he read the prayers.

He eventually closed the small book and said, "Take some slow deep breaths, concentrate on the candle flames or on the water. Either will be fine. Try to get yourselves comfortable and in a meditative state. I'm going to say a few more prayers here, to make sure we only summon spirits of light."

As I tried to get in a centered state, I struggled with my busy mind. I admitted to myself that I was glad that Allie didn't come. It would have been all too nerve wracking. I stole a glance at Rod and was surprised at how comfortable he seemed. I was glad that he grew up with a mother that practiced Spiritism. It felt so right for me. I hated to compare my previous relationships but none of them had ever included a spiritual connection. They had only been physical and often lacked an emotional connection.

My first experience attending a misa was at Hector's house for Jose before he was initiated as a child of Obatalá. Letty had been there too. It had been a lot of fun until a little too much information on my love life and ex had taken center stage. I ended up jumping up and hiding in the bathroom, hoping that they'd move the focus to someone else. Focus. That's what I had to do now, I reminded myself in an attempt to quiet all the mental noise.

Hector got Jose's attention and had him walk up to the makeshift altar. Jose stood up and cleansed himself with the water that was set in the basin before it. He seemed to smudge himself with the water. Then he knocked three times on the table with both hands. One by one we each got up to do the same thing. I was the last to do it. Next, we took Agua Florida, floral spiritual water, and freshened ourselves with it.

Ana and Hector lit cigars and sat quietly. In the darkening room, the cigar tips burned deep amber light. Realizing they were all scrying the water in the bowl on the altar, I did the same. All I saw was clear water but decided that it was okay if I didn't see anything more. This was the first misa for me and I needed to stay patient. If I stuck to this maybe one day I'd be like Hector or Ana.

Jose was the first to speak. "I'm not sure what this is but I'm seeing fish, colorful tropical ones in the water here." He squinted his eyes and tilted his head. "I'm not exactly sure what this has to do with anything but that's what I see."

"Try not to make sense of everything," Hector instructed the group. "Don't let your left brains takeover."

"There's a big Yemayá influence here." Ana sounded matter of fact. "You can feel it when you come into this apartment. You might want to explore what this means by having someone read the shells for you. I'm not trying to confuse you because this is a misa but I don't want to withhold information that is clearly for you."

Again I was reminded about Yemayá, the Orisha of the oceans. At Jose's drumming, I received a special blessing from someone who was mounted by the Orisha. I had been meaning to read some of the patakis about Yemayá but hadn't gotten around to exploring the legends as yet. Time seemed to go by so quickly.

"Are you sure this is your first misa?" Ana seemed perturbed by something. "You've been working through something, spiritually. You're very involved in the development of your spirit, although it may not seem like it. What you're doing is the not the usual, like going to church services, but I do see you in church- a lot."

I nodded. "I guess you can say that."

Most of the AA meetings I attended were held in church basements. AA wasn't a religious program at all. It was a spiritual one. This reminded me of my second step. I was supposed to start working on it by looking at how my life had become insane when I was drinking. It seemed like things had quieted down a bit but then this murder happened so close to home. I directed my attention back to the misa. Jose had started to speak.

"I'm seeing a couple swimming, no wait." Jose hesitated a bit. "No, they're scuba diving. That's what I'm seeing."

"That has to be Doctor C. and Price on their honeymoon. They were in Bermuda, not too long before he was found murdered."

"I'm starting to feel chilled." Jose visibly shivered. "It's not me. Somebody was sick. I'm not sure who it was, but someone in this triangle was sick. Sort of like the

Bermuda Triangle."

We all looked at Jose as his body started to quiver as though he had the flu. Hector took charge. "Take a minute and cleanse yourself with some of the water. Before you get up, put something on your seat. Protect yourself. There's a lot of spiritual presence here."

Jose put a white handkerchief on his seat and cleansed himself in front of the altar. "I'm better. I don't know what that was all about. I keep thinking that someone was sick. Maybe Doctor Campbell? Did anyone ever talk about that at work, Daisy?"

I hated to say what came to me. "No, sometimes there would be rumors going on, he was very active- if you know what I mean."

"Well, I'm not sure what I even mean," Jose said. "But if I were Allie, I'd get checked out."

Hector encouraged him. "Keep looking. We're not finished here. Okay, Jose?"

"Yes."

Suddenly, Rod sat straight up in his chair. I jumped.

"You've been so quiet; I almost forgot you were here."

"No, I'm here, all right," he said. "I've been sitting at tables like these for years. This isn't really new. I get this feeling that it wasn't Doctor Campbell that was ill. Definitely, Allie should get examined…"

"She will. Allie's pregnant and she wants a healthy baby, remember that's part of why we're here." For a minute I was embarrassed that Allie had wanted us to have the misa and then I hijacked it. I was worth it, though, and had been planning to have one for a while. This business with Allie had just turned up.

"Right," Rod agreed. "What I'm saying is that there was someone who was sick. I bet it was one of the patients.

I keep thinking of what you said, Daisy, about the vision of the couple arguing in the recovery room. We have to check out what happened to those patients. Did anyone of them get sick? I think we'll find something if we look a little bit deeper into that back at the hospital."

Hector interjected. "Daisy, it's true that we came here in a way for Allie but this is your misa. Don't forget that. Focus on the flame if you feel drawn to it." Hector was gentle in his reminders. "You might hear the answer from the flame." At his words, the candle hissed and the flame lengthened briefly, shining brighter.

I squinted my eyes as I saw Jose do earlier in the evening and waited. Then it dawned on me.

"Someone was about to get burned. I don't think it was Allie either. She already told them that she was pregnant. It had something to do with one of the patients. I'm with Rod here."

Hector smiled at me. "I could have told you that," he said.

I felt my cheeks burn. "I didn't mean it like that. I'm just saying that I agree with him. I think it was one of the patients, too." I turned to him. "You still have that list I gave you, don't you?"

"I gave it to my partner," Rod said. "She wanted to look it over tonight. See if she came up with anything. By bringing it into the precinct she could look to see if any of the patients were in trouble before."

"I'm confused here. I thought you saw this in the water or the fire." I was a bit disappointed.

"Both," he said as he raised his hands up defensively. "If you think I've been tricking you, I haven't been."

"Stay on track here, guys." Hector relit his cigar. "I see something here. You two are arguing about something you agree on but perceive in different ways. There's something to this. I'll bet that Doctor Campbell and the patient were doing the same thing. They agreed on something but perceived it very differently. It's almost like you two are acting it out- just like they did."

"This is weird," I said. "It's like everything has meaning here."

"I agree with that," Hector said. "Your spirits are trying to show us what happened. You can't hear them that clearly yet, but you will. You're just learning, Daisy. Keep at it and it will get clearer, the communication, I mean." He inhaled from his cigar. "There was something not right about Doctor Campbell. He was obsessed. It's like he was driven. Once he was on something he couldn't let up."

I was in definite agreement with this observation. "That's a good way to describe him."

Ana cleared her throat. "There's a spirit here. He's of a little boy. Is there any connection here?"

No one said anything so I finally did. "It might be mine." I was fearful that my personal business would come up but why wouldn't it since it was my misa?

"But it's not your child. It's a cousin or a brother."

"Yes, I don't have a child. It's my brother. He came to the last misa. Remember?"

Everyone looked up. Only those who were at the other misa knew about my brother, that meant Rod had no idea what I was talking about.

"Sometimes depending on how deep I am I don't remember. His spirit is very light… bright. He brings you flowers and sets them before you." Ana imitated what her vision showed and swept her hand out with a flourish. "They're white flowers. He wants you to know he sends you love. You should know that he was okay when he crossed over. He didn't suffer physically because he died almost instantly when he was struck by the car. He wants you to tell your father that he's okay. How is your mother? Her energy seems heavy. Why is that? Is she sick?"

"She's not in the best of shape. I don't think she'd be open to receiving this information. My mother still holds it over my father's head."

"That's part of the message too. He wants you to let your father know that it wasn't his fault. He needs to let the guilt go. Your brother shows me that he was quick as lightning and ran into the street before anyone could react. He wants you to say that."

"Thank you." A sense of lightness came over me. Although I never had the chance to meet my brother, or even knew about him until recently, he impacted my upbringing significantly.

Ana settled back in her seat and smiled. "He's been sort of a guardian angel to you. All those situations that might have been dangerous but weren't at the end of the day? You've got your big little brother to thank."

Everyone in the room smiled, imagining the small boy.

Ana took it a step further. "Do you have a bovida yet?"

"A bovida?"

"An altar with glasses of water on it for your ancestors."

"No. I have a small altar but no glasses."

Ana cackled out loud. "Hector? Falling down on the job? Why doesn't your ahijada have a bovida yet?"

"She's not my goddaughter, that's why."

"Well, what are you waiting for? A formal invitation? Here, I'll do it. Daisy, do you want Hector to be your Padrino?"

"Ana... please, this is personal..." Hector began.

"What's more personal than a misa, for goodness sakes? Daisy, what do you say?"

"I'd love it. I have been thinking about receiving my collares."

"Well, first you're going to need a rompimiento. We have to remove energy that's been tying you up, something that's not altogether nice. Do you have a boyfriend? It's strong negative male energy. Oh, wait…." Ana put her hand up. "This is personal. Make sure you two get together soon."

"Yes," Hector and I spoke in unison.

Jose smiled. "If you're going to be his goddaughter, that means I'm your big brother… your godbrother."

"That means you have to help her set up a bovida," Hector said. "Tell her what to put on her altar. Anyone have anything they'd like to add today?"

Ana asked, "Iyawó, are you still out of work?"

Jose nodded. He would be called iyawó for the entire year. It signified the importance of him being an initiate in the religion.

"I have some ideas of what you can do. We'll talk after the misa."

"Thanks, Madrina." Jose squirmed in his seat but clearly trusted his godmother.

Hector began. "Usually when someone is crowned, and the partner isn't, the partner should consider, at least, receiving beads prior to the ceremony. This didn't happen in your case, of course, because Rubio was crowned when he was a baby…"

"I think someone has their eye on you or maybe even more." Ana folded her arms across her lap. "There's an outside party who would like you two to be separate. Know what I'm talking about?"

"Not really."

"Of course, you do. There's someone who doesn't like the idea about the two of you living together. They would like to see you two apart. There's a saying about 'no se puede tener dos reyes en una casa,' two kings can't rule the same kingdom."

Rod perked up. "I've heard that. My mom has said it over the years. It means that there would be too much conflict between the two."

"Exactly," Hector said. "But in this case I don't think that's what it would mean. When you have two kings working hand in hand the power is doubled. There are certain people that would be threatened by the magnificence of such a kingdom. Think about it. You are the left brain of the operation. You have great business and financial acumen. Rubio is the right brain. He is a great artist and about to open his own gallery…"

"No, wait, he's not planning to open his own gallery…" Jose tried to interrupt. "He's hoping to sign a lease for one."

"Listen to me. I know what I'm talking about. Sometimes our spirits don't tell us what's coming down the pike until they're ready or think we're ready for something. I guarantee you that he will be having his own gallery. A successful one. If someone suspects that the glow from your two crowns together would be too bright you don't know what lengths they'd go to get you two separated. Rubio's coming home late? Distant? That's not the Rubio we know. Tell him I'd like to see him."

"I will. I appreciate this." Jose took a deep breath. "It's a lot of information to take in."

"But how did you know?" I asked Hector.

"I told you the first time you consulted with me. Trust your intuition. Anything else?" Hector looked around the room. No one moved. "I think we should start ending this."

Wait," I said, "we're not closer to finding out what happened than we were before tonight. What are we going to tell Allie?"

"I know you'd like to sit here longer but this type of work doesn't happen because you want to will it to happen." Hector clipped the end of his cigar and set it at the side of the ashtray. It was a relic from my cigarette and alcohol driven days. "If you are supposed to get information you do. You just can't go behind the veils and get all the answers you'd like. This isn't a novela. This is real. Time takes time. Remember that."

"You sound like my mother, Hector," Rod said. "She always said that type of stuff. Maybe that's why I'm a detective now."

Hector chuckled and directed us onto the next step, "We can start cleansing ourselves."

One by one, just as at the beginning of the misa, we cleansed ourselves and paid homage to the altar.

"You need a good cleaning. Come here." Hector took me by the hand and stood me in front of him. He took a branch of lucky leaves, some flowers and blew cigar smoke over them. Then he poured cologne over them. He twirled me around as he smudged me with the bouquet. Once completed, he broke the branches and left them on the floor in front of the altar.

Hector indicated I should sit down while each participant was cleaned and smudged in the same way. When everyone was finished we all began singing a song and twirling in a circle thanking the spirits for their help and then we sent them on their way. I hadn't thought about that song since the first misa I attended but easily remembered it when Hector and Ana began singing. Once the living room was cleaned up and the water discarded, we all stood around the living room.

"I'm starved," Ana said and took a quick peek into the kitchen. "What's cooking?"

"I made lasagna. Just give me a minute to brown the bread. I'm about to pop it into the oven."

A short while later we were all satiated from the delicious meal and exhausted from the spiritual session.

"I always say this is the best part of a misa," Rod said. "The meal was fabulous."

"I guess I should be heading downstairs," Jose said. "Rubio should be home soon."

"Like I said, contact me." Hector embraced his godson and gave him blessings. He turned to me. "Do you have any feathers?"

"Feathers? For what? I don't understand."

"They're a great tool for smudging," he said. "This is Cleansing Energy Field 101. Be on the lookout. If you find any, they're probably for you."

"Where am I going to find feathers, other than chicken? I never even see those in Brooklyn." My practical side showed itself. "This is Park Slope, not the Poconos."

"If it's meant to be, you'll get them no matter where you are."

Jose and Hector walked into the hallway and made their way down the steps after quick good byes. Rod and I looked at each other as we stood in the doorway.

"Daisy..." he started.

I placed my hand on his chest to stop him. "I didn't mean to question you about the patient list. I know this is your job... I'm just working through stuff."

"Stuff?" Rod smiled a bit. "Stuff. I like that. What's stuff?"

"Let's go back inside," I said. "There are some things I'd like you to know about me."

Rod linked his arm through mine and we retreated into the living room. We sat down on the couch and Ms. G. sprang onto his lap.

"Do you want some tea or something? Herbal?"

"Are you stalling? I'm stuffed," he said. "And that reminds me that I want to hear about stuff."

I shook my head slightly. "I'm not as sane as you think I am. I don't mean I'm a nut. What I mean is that I need to take things slow. This is my first year."

"Your first year?" he asked. "First year of what? Sorry, I don't get what you're trying to say."

I plunged in. "I used to drink pretty heavily. I decided I couldn't do that to myself anymore. I was pretty sick. I don't really want to get into those things now, maybe another time. Right now, I just want to tell you that... I'm sober."

"Sober? Okay..."

"It's just that now that I'm not drinking, my issues are always coming up."

"You and the rest of the world have issues, Daisy." Rod laughed gently. He took my hand and intertwined his fingers with mine. "Don't worry; I knew there was something up when I noticed that you didn't order a mojito at the restaurant the other night. Mojito palace."

"You don't care?" I was bewildered.

"I wouldn't say that I don't care. What I mean is, I know that some people can drink and some can't." He smiled warmly at me. "I know all about that in the work I do. I don't want to tell you how much crime happens because someone is soused or just had one too many."

I had a flash of the image of Lou and me the night we both had just one too many. I closed my eyes. That was something I didn't want to talk about tonight with Rod. I wasn't proud of the fact that I allowed myself to be Lou's recipient of rage for a while.

"Thanks, I'm glad you understand." I cringed at the thought that those were the only words I could muster.

"I want to know about you," he said. "I told you that before." He lightly kissed the tips of my fingers. "This okay?"

I nodded because I couldn't trust myself to speak. Having my fingers kissed in this way was not something that I was used to. Keeping my eyes closed, I allowed myself to let the delicious feeling go from my fingers through my body. I settled deeper into the cushions. It just felt so good. Rod took my other hand and did the same. My breath became heavier as he kissed my fingers and then my wrists. There was a knock at the door.

I opened my eyes and sat up. "What?"

Hector's voice came through the door. "Sorry, Daisy, I forgot my lighter."

The electricity I felt through my body a moment earlier dissipated. "Oh, I see it." Stooping to pick it up from the coffee table, I retrieved it, and brought it to the door. Opening it, I handed the lighter to Hector.

"Thanks," he said. "Have a good night. Don't forget, give me a call tomorrow."

"Sure, no problem." I closed the door once more behind me. I turned to see Rod had stood up. "Leaving?"

"Yeah," he said. "I've got an early morning."

"Oh, okay… me too…" I felt so awkward.

Rod stood in front of me and shoved his hands in his pockets. He looked so vulnerable and serious at the same time.

"The truth is that I'm leaving early because I don't want to rush things with us. I think we need to go slow. We don't need to do anything to ruin this."

"Ruin this?" I was startled. "Did I do something?"

"No," Rod said. "You know what they say; good things come to those who wait."

"Isn't that a stupid cliché?" I put my hand back on the door knob.

"There's a difference between stupid clichés, as you put it, and sayings that actually mean something. They've meant something to people for years- for a reason."

"I guess you're right." I thought of all the slogans at the twelve step meetings I thought were just written to placate the angry mob of drinkers. 'Live and let live.' 'Easy Does It.' That one made a lot of sense here with Rod. "See, I told you I have issues. I see what you mean. Will you be at the hospital tomorrow?"

"We might not," he said. "We're probably going to follow up on some leads based on the patient list you gave us. Munroe said she was going to use part of today to pick out the priority people that we need to question."

"Why do you think anyone would want to hurt Doctor Price?" I asked just as Rod was about to leave.

"That, I think, we'll find out when we find Doctor Campbell's murderer."

Before he left, Rod held me lightly at my waist. He smiled and kissed me fully on the lips. The electricity overcame my body as I felt his being invite me to him but then I felt him pull back and with his forehead against mine, he cradled my face with his hands. "Like I said, I don't want to do anything to ruin us," he whispered.

The smell of his aftershave was a heady mix of cinnamon and apples. Rod kissed me once more on the lips and I savored the moment. We stepped back from each other simultaneously.

"Good night." Rod headed down the steps and I went back into my apartment.

Damned murder case.

Chapter 16

The number of media vans parked outside the entrance at Windsor Medical Center was less than it had been in several days. A prominent lawyer, who had a rumored connection with organized crime, was shot on his way home as he exited his SUV. The event took place in Manhattan and captured the media's attention. Dr. Campbell's and Price's deaths had become yesterday's news. In a way I was glad about that because getting into the facility had become that much easier. I didn't have to deal with reporters hounding the entrance or worry that they would figure out my position at the hospital. It only took me a few moments to get to my office.

Sophia and I scrutinized the list on the work table in front of us once again.

"It's got to be Garden Stills. She's the one who had a problem in the O.R. that afternoon. The code was called for her," I said with all certainty.

"That may be true but how can we know for sure? We just can't go knocking on her door. Can we?"

"No." I thought for a few minutes. "We can do a courtesy call, though. We can tell her that we wanted to catch up and make sure that everything was all right… or something like that."

"I don't want to get us into deeper trouble than we're in already, Daisy. I'm not too happy about cold calling her."

"You won't. I will. I admitted her that day. I can tell her that I wanted to touch base with her to see how's she's doing. I know her from before. It's not the first cosmetic surgery that she's had done at the hospital."

"I think you're going way out on a limb here. What

do you expect her to say? That she killed Doctor Campbell when she climbed down from her gurney. That it happened straight out of the operating room?"

"No, I guess it doesn't sound too realistic when you put it like that."

"What's driving you? What's making you think that Stills is going to give you any information?"

"It's a gut feeling. It may turn out to be nothing. But then again it might turn us toward another lead."

"Us? Are we the detectives now?"

There was no reason to start antagonizing Sophia but she was the one who brought out all those folders and had us both go through them with a fine tooth comb. Suddenly, she was getting cold feet. There was something to this.

"Can I ask you something?" I decided to tread lightly.

Sophia took her reading glasses off. "Go ahead, although I do reserve the right not to answer."

"That's what I mean. It seemed like you wanted to know who did this. Two people that were pretty close to you or at least the hospital you represent are dead. Why back out now? Is there something you're not telling me?"

"Absolutely not... this sounds ridiculous if you ask me, and to imply that I don't want to catch the person that did this is offensive. I just don't want to open up another can of worms."

"You won't be. I will. Let me try to contact Ms. Stills and see if anything comes up. If nothing does, then no harm done and we just leave it alone."

"Just this one. I don't think I can agree to you contacting anyone else on the list."

"You may not have to."

The penthouse apartment overlooked Prospect Park. The windows were bathed in white billowy curtains. The rest of the furnishings were spare but the walls were covered with artwork. There were pieces ranging from 1960's psychedelic forms to dark medieval paintings. I had no idea who the artists were but I knew they were talented. Everything was very beautiful. They varied in theme and the placements on the walls showed them all off to their best advantage. It was easy to see that someone loved art in this household.

"You have a lovely home, ma'am." I stood near the window. "And your view is spectacular. I live near the park and spend a bit of my time there but this is really something."

"Thank you, dear. I fell in love with the view when my husband and I moved in many years ago." Mrs. Stills placed the lilies that I brought her into a vase and set them on the table behind the couch. "How did you know that I love lilies?"

"I love them too. I remember the last time you were hospitalized; your husband filled your room with them." I winced inside when I realized what I just said. It might not be the best thing to remind the lady of her multiple cosmetic surgeries. She looked fabulous though.

"I do remember. You were very sweet to me that time. You didn't have to make those phone calls for me. You also made sure that Doctor Hagar came down to check that swelling before I left. The nurses were so busy that day. I hate to admit that I was feeling quite insecure."

"Wow, I almost don't remember all that. That all happened a couple of years ago, didn't it?" I was slightly embarrassed to be having this conversation. It was proof that my memory was still like Swiss cheese; full of holes.

"That was when I had the breast augmentation, but I'd rather not go into it right now. What can I do for you? Why are you here?"

Mrs. Stills was gracious. How could I get the information without seeming like a big snoop? Being truthful might be the only way to go about it.

"I had some questions about what happened to you in the Operating Room. I know it's none of my business but I keep wondering…"

"Whether I killed Dr. Campbell?"

I was struck by her candor.

"Let me make this easy for you." Mrs. Stills strode across her living room and closed the double pocket doors to the foyer.

Shrinking back a bit, not knowing what to expect, I felt like a worm. Sophia had been right. I didn't belong here delving into this woman's personal business.

"I'm sharing this as much for me as for you. I didn't kill Doctor Campbell." She shook her head slightly and smiled. She looked so engaging. Her short reddish hair was in an old fashioned Vidal Sassoon style that I had seen in magazines. Mrs. Stills could have been nineteen years old if you squinted just a bit. "I didn't do anything to hurt him. I was afraid of him."

"You, afraid of Doctor Campbell?" Her admission surprised me. He could be a jerk but who would be fearful of him?

"We knew each other years ago. We met when we were in college. This was all before he went on to medical school and I became an art appraiser." She swept her arm toward the wall. "It's mere coincidence that we live in the same area, or I should say lived because I won't have to see him anymore."

I watched a kaleidoscope of emotions shift through

Mrs. Stills' facial expressions. My gut told me to keep quiet.

"Do you know what it's like to see your rapist at church? Or to pass his house when you park your car, wondering if he's inside, or if he's lurking in your building vestibule?" Her mouth curled in disgust. "Yes, that's been my life for many years. I've also watched his sons grow up. His son, Ted, was in nursery school with my daughter, Pia."

"Oh, Mrs. Stills, I'm sorry... I had no idea. I should never have come." I began to stand up to leave there as quickly as possible.

"No, I'd like to finish." She raised her hand to stop me. "I've never shared any of this with the police. I don't know if I will. What happened to me, happened a long time ago. As I said I knew him in college. We never dated, but that didn't stop him from taking an interest in me... a sexual one."

I could hear the controlled anger in her voice.

"Sit down, please. Relax, dear. It's not like you've brought up something new. I've wrestled with this since my co-ed days.

"Yes, ma'am." I was at a loss. Now I knew what Sophia had meant when she warned me about opening up a can of worms. This was some can.

"We only went out in groups those days. My parents expected me to be very ladylike. I was responsible for making sure that I would not get into any sort of trouble. It was the early seventies. There was lots of trouble to be had. I was a child and I wanted to be like the others." Her voice softened but I could still hear the resentment in her tone. "My parents were ensconced in our big house in Connecticut. They had no idea what was going on. Don't get me wrong. They knew very well what the kids were doing but never expected me to be one of 'the kids.' I had very high standards to maintain."

I could definitely relate. Our lives might have been completely different but our parents' expectations were pretty similar. Maintain yourself above everyone else without any direction from them. Both sets of parents probably had a hands-off approach. For both of us that meant falling into harm's way. I listened on as Mrs. Stills continued to speak.

"We somehow managed to keep our grades up but we had keg parties practically every weekend. That night there was a frat party. I went with one of my sorority sisters. Someone invariably showed up with marijuana and L.S.D. That night was like every other night we got together." She paused and took a breath trying to push the heaviness of the memories away. "I wish I had never partaken. I thought I was a grown up, holding a can of beer, and smoking pot."

Mrs. Stills sat next to me on the couch and patted my hand. "I'm glad you showed up today, dear. The memories have been eating away at me since the surgery. He slipped something into my beer that night ... I woke up in the middle of the night with him pulling my skirt down. These days, they call it rape... but in those days... it was a no fuss, no muss, just keep quiet..." She shuddered.

"I'm sorry." I wasn't quite sure what else to say but felt I had to say something. The fact that she confided something so serious to me was totally unexpected. I didn't think that my simple act of kindness would lead her to tell me what I was sure to be the most horrendous event of her life. This must have been weighing heavily on her mind.

"It's okay. There's nothing to be done today. All of this happened a very long time ago. I thought I had gotten over it. He was walking right outside my door one morning… you see, I never got help. At the time I felt I there was no one to tell. My parents would have disowned me. But after seeing him I went to therapy and worked on how I would handle seeing him again."

"But it wasn't your fault," I said.

"I thought it was. I should never have been out there drinking with a bunch of college boys. I honestly thought it was my mistake. With everything that's been happening I know now that it was his fault. He did it. I didn't do anything to seduce him on. In fact, I ignored him. I had this crazy crush on one of the other boys who couldn't give me the time of day."

"What happened in the recovery room?" My curiosity was getting the best of me.

"I expected to see Doctor Hagar there. He's my surgeon. I'm very happy with his work and trust him. He didn't come to see me before the surgery but I implicitly knew that he would be there. I never expected to wake up and see Arthur standing over me on the stretcher. I was still under the effect of anesthesia and didn't know whether what I was seeing was real or a dream. My heart started to beat very fast and I couldn't catch my breath…"

I thought back to that afternoon. "That's when the code was called…"

"Yes. I'm still foggy as to the details. The medical team called it a 'hypotensive moment' once I was stabilized. I think it was more that I was having the fright of my life."

"Did he know how you felt about him? Why would Doctor Campbell perform surgery on you after what happened so many years ago?"

"I don't even think he realized who I was. I understand he changed shifts with Doctor Hagar. It was that simple, really. I never meant anything to him. He probably didn't remember my name. But I remembered his, quite well."

"So, him being killed on the same night that all this happened is merely a coincidence?"

"Yes. I must say I'm not surprised that someone had it in for him. Although what happened to me was a long time ago, I'm sure that his ruthless behavior has made him many enemies since then."

"Thank you for being so honest with me, I know that you didn't have to do this."

"As I said earlier, Daisy, you have been quite nice to me," Mrs. Stills said. "And once again, you've been very nice to me today. Thank you for listening."

A few minutes after leaving the lavishly built home, I was standing on Prospect Park West. A walk in the park would do me good, I thought. I needed to think some of this through before heading back to work. As I entered the park, I took a deep breath. I needed to do some soul searching. My relationship with Dr. Campbell had been brief but I had to admit that I'd been lucky. That guy had trouble with him. After being with Lou I'd been too quick when I jumped into dating Dr. C. It was as though I had a broken pointer. I couldn't pick out the right type of guy it seemed. Now I was seeing Rod. I began to ask myself what did I know about him, really? I wondered if I was back to my old self trying to fill that empty void in my life. Ever since I could remember, I allowed myself to get into the wrong types of relationships out of fear of being alone. Angela called them 'character defects' and she had me working on Steps One to Three. Later on in the program I'd explore more of my character defects, those things that stood between me and a sober way of life. In the meantime, I decided to take it slow with Rod. He was right, there was no need to rush.

I walked along the avenue until I came upon the Third Street entrance and passed the beautiful Litchfield Villa. Lingering flowers beckoned me into the garden that surrounded the mansion. I was reminded, once again, that I wanted to help Marge to resurrect her backyard. There was still time for cleaning up the area and for planting tulip and hyacinth bulbs that would be lovely in the spring. It would be my first garden. Well, maybe it really wasn't mine but Marge had been happy when I showed interest in the garden. I promised myself that I would work on it the following Saturday. Maybe I could rope Jose into helping out. I giggled with the thought of him kneeling down handling potting soil while wearing white. As I walked toward my house I was feeling better about myself. This walk did a world of good for me.

❁

Arriving back at home I let myself in through the second floor entrance. I looked at myself in the mirror that took up the length of the foyer. Not too bad. My skin was clearer and my cheeks were rosier than they'd been since I was a kid. I noticed that my long wavy locks were vibrating with health, shining, and thick. My hair was the one thing I always took pride in. Further checking myself out, I turned around and noticed that my pants were a bit more snug. I had struggled with putting on weight for a while but over the past year there was finally some meat on my bones. No more feeling embarrassed at how thin I looked in my clothes. This sobriety thing had its perks.

"*Mirror, mirror, on the wall, who's...*" Jose came down the steps and stood next to me. We gazed at our reflections.

"*...and you're the fairest of them all!* I don't believe it. You look great!" I was surprised at the drastic change in his appearance. He wore one of his light grey business suits. The white outfit and skull cap were gone. "What does it feel like? Being in regular clothes again?"

"I don't feel good about it but it's something I have to do. I spoke with Hector after the misa and he reminded me that he gave me permission to wear my suits before I got crowned. I told you already that I'm a stickler for tradition."

"What does this mean? Are you going on an interview? That's the only thing it could mean."

"No. I'm not going on an interview." Jose folded his arms and looked me up and down. "Where are you coming from?"

"Don't change the subject on me," I said. "We're talking about you. If you're not going on an interview than where are you going?"

"Ha! I just got back from one. I heard you coming in so I came back down the stairs." Jose seemed elated. "I knew something was going to change after that misa. I could feel it. I got a call the next morning for my first interview in a couple of months."

"And? Did you get the job?" I couldn't keep still I was so happy for him. "This is so exciting, Jose, I mean, Iyawó."

"Funny, aren't you? I don't know yet. They said they'll contact me about a second interview within a couple of days, the latest before the week is out."

"I'm so glad for you, wow, finally!"

"Put a prayer out there in the universe for me, please," he said seriously. "So, where are you coming from?"

"You're not going to believe this. I did a little sleuthing for Sophia. She's really upset about the murders. I never thought she'd go for it but she let me go out to Mrs.

Stills' house... she was one of the patients that day. I got the scoop on what happened to her when she got sick at the hospital and the short answer is no, she isn't the murderer."

"Sure about that? What would Rod or his partner think about her? Just because she said she wasn't the murderer doesn't mean that she isn't. Practically speaking, not too many people admit to being a killer- especially to a secretary. You're not even the fuzz."

"Thanks a lot. Just to clarify things, I'm not a secretary. I'm the assistant to the administrator. Got that?"

"That wouldn't make her admit to having killed Doctor Campbell." He reminded me that I might have been quick to discard her motive. "Was she another of his sweethearts?"

"No, she was definitely not his sweetheart. They were about as compatible as Birkenstocks and white socks."

"There's a whole generation of people who'd tell you that Birkenstocks and white socks go great together," Jose quipped.

"Maybe I gave a bad example. According to Sophia, Doctor C. and Price were most certainly not a happy couple. I wouldn't be surprised if she killed him and someone came along and did her in."

"Why are we talking about the doctors? I wanted to know more about Mrs. Stills. Why did you go to see her? Was she really a suspect?"

"I kind of feel like I would be breaking a confidentiality agreement if I were to tell you what she said today."

"Daisy, did she ask you to keep her information to yourself? Because if she did, I get it, if she didn't, why are you holding out on me?"

"You're right. I'm just a bit uncomfortable with the

whole thing but I can tell you, I guess. It's not like you're going to broadcast it."

"Daisy…"

"I'm telling you what she said. Hold your horses, okay. It seems that they knew each other in college and she says that he raped her, that's the bottom line. She recognized him but Mrs. Stills isn't sure that Doctor C. knew who she was when they were at the hospital that day."

"I bet there's more to the story that she's not telling you. I bet Price was blackmailing Mrs. Stills," Jose instigated. "She knew that if the information on what Doctor Campbell did got out that her reputation would be destroyed."

"Her reputation? Are you for real? Who cares about that?"

"A lot of people do. Their reputations are the most important things they have, especially when they come from old money, like these people do."

I felt a sobriety flash. "I get it. I spent so many years just trying to fit in or be someone that people would like that I didn't give my reputation much thought."

Jose was on a roll. "A woman in Mrs. Stills' position gives reputation great thought. Think about her being a young woman just starting college. It must have been very exciting for her. It was the seventies. Come on, she was a trendsetter. Doctor Campbell took something very important away from her but, all that said, I don't think she's the murderer."

"I don't think so either." I agreed with his logic.

"But, we can be pretty sure that the murderer knew him. He or she must have. Strangers can't get into the O.R. suite, can they?"

"With a code going on anything is possible. The

killer could have come in at that point and hidden to catch him."

"Where does your 'pixie lady' fit in… if anywhere here?"

We both thought about it for a few minutes.

"I have no idea. I'm kind of tired of thinking. Enough is enough." I walked over to the door. "Let's go see if Marge is baking something. I'm starved and can't wait for dinner. I also want to talk to her about planting bulbs in her yard. What about you? Want to pitch in?"

"Why not? It'll keep me busy while I wait for a call back for the second interview. First, I need to go and cleanse myself off and jump back into my whites. See you in a few."

"Okay."

Chapter 17

The next morning, I was back at my desk. I pushed folders and documents aside so I could take a swig from my latte. Concentrating on my work was next to impossible. I had to tell Sophia exactly what Mrs. Stills told me but I was uneasy about it. Mrs. Stills hadn't emphasized that what she shared was a secret but it might hurt her if too many people got wind of her ordeal. It was hard for me to deal with this information for one day; I couldn't have imagined living with it for decades. I really needed to consider Jose's talk about reputation. I didn't want anyone to get hurt.

Sophia Cornelius flounced in wearing a solid grey outfit that outlined her more than ample body. All she needed was an orange accessory of some sort and she'd look exactly like an African Grey parrot. It was obvious from her swagger that she was on a power trip today and that could mean just about anything.

"Good morning, dear." Sophia picked the mail up from my desk. "Anything you'd like to share? I figure there is since you didn't come in after your meeting with Mrs. Stills yesterday."

"I left her apartment about two-thirty. I guess I could have come back... I'm sorry. It didn't occur to me. I had a good view of the park from her windows and all I could think of was going into the park and clearing my head."

"And did you?" Sophia's smile resembled a grimace.

"Yes... I mean... no... I don't know... I don't know what happened. The autumn colors looked gorgeous and I felt pulled towards the park. That's all. I took a long walk."

"A long walk?"

"Yes, a long walk. I think you should do the same sometime. It can do wonders for you. My head was clearer and my heart, I'm sure, is beating stronger because of it. Doing some sort of exercise is next on my agenda. I'm not going to be young forever..."

"Daisy, please, the update."

"It's a long story..."

"Well, we're here until five, go ahead, we have plenty of time."

To make sure no one heard what I was going to say, I led the way into Sophia's office and closed the door behind us. I took a deep breath and dove into sharing Mrs. Stills' account of what took place the day of the code and what happened all those years ago with Doctor C. I was glad at the end of it when Sophia advised me that we would keep this all quiet. She made the point that it was no one's business what occurred in Mrs. Stills' personal life when she was a young girl. It was up to Mrs. Stills to make the choice of who would come to know and when. Her past experiences weren't for us to tell.

The rest of the day was eerily quiet. I didn't hear from Rod or Letty. I was forced to sit and deal with my feelings about everything, especially the mysterious nature of the two murders of colleagues I had come to know pretty well, even if it was after their deaths.

"Sophia, I'm about to leave, is that it for today? I made the printouts for tomorrow's Power Point presentation. I.T. will have the connections up tomorrow. They'll be here at nine and your meeting is scheduled for two. This way if I.T. has a lame excuse for being late it won't interrupt your meeting." I stood waiting for a signal from Sophia, instead the phone rang.

Sophia nodded and I picked it up. "Mrs. Campbell," I mouthed again and waited for Sophia's okay to hand her the phone. I wondered what the urgency was now at the end of the day.

She listened for a few minutes before responding. "That's wonderful news, Charlotte. Sometimes boys at that age rebel when they're unable to discharge their emotional feelings. It was a terrible loss for him." She silently listened to Mrs. Campbell on the other end. "I'm sure that Charles will come out of it. He's in shock. I'm sure that's why he hasn't contacted you. He's using his work as a place to bury his feelings." Sophia looked at me and shrugged. "Very well. Tonight? You're sure of this? Are you ready to return to work so soon? This won't be a problem at all. Hold on a minute, please."

Sophia put the call on hold. "Daisy, would you mind running some papers over to Mrs. Campbell?"

"Sure." What choice did I have? We all lived in the same area.

"I'll have Daisy bring them over in about an hour. Yes, my assistant. As long as you're ready to return to work, we're here to help you do just that." She replaced the phone receiver down on the cradle.

"An hour?" I had hoped to get home early enough to veg out in front of the television. My schedule had been so hectic that it seemed I never had the time to either curl up with a good book or watch a T.V. show. Even a walk around the park was out of the question. It was getting darker earlier each day.

"I do apologize, dear. I never expected her to be ready to return to work this soon. The problem is that we need her signatures on original papers. Scanning and downloading won't work in this case. It's very important that she signs them. We're way behind. We've been in a financial crisis of sorts since the double murders." Sophia hesitated, took her glasses off, and rubbed at her eyes. "Opening up a new ambulatory clinic was already a risky project because of Park Hill. We have stiff competition from their camp. They've been stable for years now. We have to take more risks in order to stay in the game. Mrs. Campbell is the chair of the board of trustees and her recent lack of involvement is dangerous. I hope you don't mind doing this."

"It's okay. I was probably going to fall asleep in front of some trashy reality T.V. show anyway. I didn't have much planned for this evening," I joked as my longed for vision of wearing my pajamas on the couch while eating a giant bowl of popcorn was getting smaller and smaller. Maybe I'd try meditating when I got home instead. It was always a toss-up.

"Take your jacket off then. Is there anything more you can do while you wait for me to complete these papers? It'll be a while. Our lawyer had given them to me but with all the commotion I haven't looked at them. They have to be perfect before you run them over to Mrs. Campbell."

"I'll wait outside in my office." Back at my desk, I saw that I missed a phone call from Rod. "I'm going to make a few phone calls while I wait for you to read through that, okay?"

"Yes, yes," Sophia muttered as she opened a large manila folder on her desk.

I pressed callback and Rod answered on the first ring. "Hey, what would you say about meeting for dinner? I'm in the neighborhood."

"Sorry, I can't."

"I didn't mean that I only wanted to meet with you because I was around the hospital. I did try you earlier. I had no idea what my schedule was going to be like. I'm finishing up a lot earlier than…"

"It's not you. It's me. I would have said yes about three minutes ago. Trust me. I'd love to meet up with you. It's just that I found out that I'll be working later than I planned to," I said, lowering my voice. "Sophia has me here waiting on some papers. I have to deliver them to Charlotte Campbell. Muñiz courier, at your service."

"How about if I call you later on? When I'm done with work? It's not even six. Maybe we can go out for dessert or something? Or I could pick something up and bring it over?"

"I like that idea."

"Okay, just give me a call later when you're done for the day?"

I realized that I was smiling through the entire phone call. I felt so many unchartered feelings rushing in whenever I spoke to him. Did I really think about taking things slowly? What was wrong with me?

About a half hour later, Sophia called me from her inner office. "Daisy, come in and pick this up. It's ready to go. Just remember to wait for the signatures and you can bring it back in the morning. No need to come back here tonight."

"Are you sure that this is it for tonight?" I really didn't want to stay any longer but since I left early the day before I should try to rectify forgetting to come back to the office.

"Yes, I'm sure. It's been a long day. Have a good night, dear, and thanks for taking these papers."

The temperature had dropped and the evening was quite cool. I was glad that I had my thick shawl to throw over my jacket. I wouldn't be outside for too long, before I knew it I'd be at home with Rod… talk about looking forward to warmth.

My heels were killing me as I made my way to President Street. It never occurred to me that I should have slipped on the running shoes that I kept hidden under my desk. It was dark and a chill went up my spine and my feet hurt with each step that I took. This errand was becoming my personal hell. "This is what happens when I forget to return to the office," I muttered to myself.

The Campbell manor was up ahead. I took a deep breath and slowed my pace. I didn't want to them to see me out of breath with my teeth chattering. That wasn't the look I was trying to cultivate. I stopped in front of the house. The upper floor windows were lit and the second floor landing was well illuminated showing off a gleaming heavy oak door. I climbed the stairs and rang the bell.

As in most of the prestigious homes in the area, there were no window coverings. The owners seemed to take a pride in letting all passersby peek into their magnificent homes. While I waited for someone to open the door, I couldn't help but look through the front windows into the house. There were several people in the parlor. Ted was standing close to the window and I pulled back a bit. I thought it would be better not to have him look into my eyes; it was awkward enough but it seemed I was spying on them. Suddenly, the door opened.

"Yes?" A middle aged woman with short auburn hair stood there. She wore casual dress slacks and button down shirt.

"I'm Daisy Muñiz from Windsor Medical Center. I've brought some papers for Mrs. Campbell to sign. She's expecting me, I mean, them," I said, holding up the envelope that Sophia gave me.

"Please come in." The woman stepped back into the

vestibule and motioned for me to follow. This was the first time I'd been in the house. It was splendid. It outshone the lavish home Dr. Campbell and Price had renovated. The difference here was that the house looked just as it probably did the century earlier when it was built. It was wide, unlike many of the Brooklyn brownstones. The woodwork that covered the walls glowed. The crystal chandelier had to be unique, I thought. I marveled at the crystals that were shaped like teardrops. The parquet floors were elaborately designed. In some areas they were covered with rugs someone had obviously picked out with care and love. The woman indicated that I should sit down.

"Thank you." I sat on a small settee near the flowing staircase that led to the upper floors. The door to the parlor was open and the family somehow looked to me like actors performing on a stage. Each stood in his or her place as though ready to read their lines. Ted was standing between Mrs. Campbell and another woman whose back was towards me. I saw the roaring fireplace and yearned for its warmth. The same woman who opened the door, who must have been a maid or a housekeeper, gave Mrs. Campbell the envelope I handed to her with the documents.

Mrs. Campbell perused the documents quickly. She accepted a pen from the petite auburn haired woman and signed her name with a flourish. As she placed the papers back into the manila envelope, the woman who stood in front of the marble fireplace turned toward me, looking directly at me. It was the pixie! There stood the woman who came in looking for Dr. Campbell the night of his murder.

I lowered my eyes. It was confusing and I didn't want to make eye contact with her- at least not yet. As the housekeeper brought the manila envelope back to me, the pixie walked out of the parlor and grabbed a paisley shawl from the coat rack that stood in the hallway. She left the house in a hurry, calling back at Mrs. Campbell.

"Don't obsess about this, Charlotte. I'll be back in a bit."

The voice was the same. The lyrical sound wasn't one that was easy to forget. But what was she doing here of all places? I was surprised but realized that there wasn't any reason for the woman not to be at the Campbell house; when I first saw her, she came in looking for Dr. Campbell.

I took the envelope, thanked the housekeeper, and began to leave. I needed to follow the mysterious pixie, it was the only way that I could find out who she was and her connection to the family. In my haste, I dropped the envelope and as I tried to retrieve it, I heard Mrs. Campbell calling out.

"Megan, don't let the assistant leave. I'd like that envelope back. I forgot to make copies. Please scan the documents."

"Yes ma'am." Megan dutifully took the envelope back out of my hands. "Have a seat, please. This will take a few minutes."

I did as I was told but my mind was on the woman who didn't seem to stay in one place for very long. I finally caught up with her and in just a matter of moments she was gone again. Maybe I could pick something up psychically while I waited. The possibility of receiving some images was not that farfetched. This was Dr. Campbell's ex-wife's house after all; he had to come here to pick Ted up. The young woman also had a connection with Dr. Campbell.

I took a deep cleansing breath and saw Rubio, of all people, in my mind's eye. Why him? He was signing some papers. In the visualization, there were a few other men, wearing tuxedos, sitting around the desk he leaned over. In the corner of the vision was a beautiful woman who sipped a martini. Her smile was cunning. The woman's dark glittering eyes matched the diamond necklace around her neck. Rubio finished signing the papers and picked up a champagne glass. The group toasted the transaction.

"Miss Muñiz, I'm sorry that you've had to wait so long. I realize that your work day ended a couple of hours ago."

I opened my eyes and there was Mrs. Campbell standing in front of me. I smiled at her while hoping that I wouldn't forget the vision I just had. "This isn't any trouble at all. I wanted to let you know that I feel terrible about your family's loss. We all respected Doctor Campbell a great deal at the hospital."

"You knew him?" Mrs. Campbell looked over her shoulder and then walked over to the parlor doors and closed them behind her. She spoke in a low voice. "I don't want Ted to get upset. Whenever we talk about his father he becomes distraught. He adored his father."

"Yes, I know that Ted was missing for a few days."

"Yes, he went to stay with a relative. He's home now and that is what's important. We're waiting for his older brother, Charles, to come home. He's been away for far too long now."

This might be my one opportunity to find out who the pixie was. "Mrs. Campbell, the young lady who just left the house a few minutes ago…"

"The young lady…?"

Mrs. Campbell shook her head. At that moment, Megan came in from another door with the envelope.

"They're scanned. You can take them with you."

I took the envelope from Megan and wasn't sure if I should pursue trying to get information about the mystery woman.

Suddenly, Mrs. Campbell answered my question.

"Of course, the young woman, that's Sybille, Sybille O'Connor, my son, Charles's fiancée. She's staying with us for a while. Charles has been busy with his work. Why, do you know her, too?"

"No, I just confused her with someone else, but I don't know any O' Connors. Well, I guess, I'd better be on my way. Thank you. Have a good evening, Mrs. Campbell."

I couldn't wait to leave and call Rod. He'd be happy to learn the identity of the mystery woman. Sybille O'Connor. I finally had a name for my pixie lady and her connection to Dr. Campbell. Sybille, his son's fiancée.

"Rod, it's me. You have to call me right back. Something interesting just happened." I called him and left a message the minute I stepped onto the stoop of the Campbell home.

Holding onto the bannister, I made my way down the stairs and started to open the gate. There was a huge grinning pumpkin placed on the bottom step. My eyes traveled to the tree that took up the front patch of garden. It was lit with orange lights and several shadowy and ghost-like apparitions waved in the air. They were probably there for Ted. He was still a child or at least had been before his father's death forced him into an abrupt maturity. As I fumbled with the intricate gate lock, I noticed a car parked directly in front of the house.

Sybille sat in the driver's seat. The woman who I began to think was a ghost since she disappeared after her brief Sixth Saturday appearance was now a few yards away from where I stood. I grasped the lock firmly and let myself out of the small enclosed yard.

"Excuse me!" I tried to capture her attention. She was peering down onto her own smartphone and the light illuminated her features. I recognized the large blue eyes and high cheekbones that I saw that fateful afternoon.

Sybille stared up at me through the closed window, seemingly having no recognition of ever having set eyes on me.

"We met before… at the hospital…"

She cracked the window open about a half inch. "I'm sorry. I'm late for an appointment. I have to be on my way," she said, closing the window and pulling the car out of the spot.

I stood there staring at the taillights when I saw a figure coming straight toward me. This time I decided to listen to my intuition that was signaling me strongly and moved behind an enormous sycamore tree. Something told me it was best not to be seen.

I held onto the tree trunk and took some deep breaths, anything to keep me from collapsing. The figure looming close to me was that of Dr. Campbell. I thought my eyes were playing tricks on me. How could it be him? He was dead. My phone began to vibrate in my jacket pocket and I struggled not to answer it. I couldn't pull it out right then. He would hear me make noise from where I stood hidden in the dark. I ducked low to decrease the chances of him seeing me. It was so confusing to see him walk through the gate that I had just come from.

Dr. Campbell let himself into the first floor. The lights were off and I couldn't see inside. This had to be the only apartment on the block that wasn't lit for miles around. Many first floor units in brownstones were used as separate garden apartments. As I stared off into the darkness I wondered what the Campbell family was hiding and why was Dr. Campbell alive?

Chapter 18

The sight of Dr. Campbell was jarring. I stood behind the tree trying to make sense of what I'd just seen. It couldn't be him, I reasoned with myself. He was dead. I had just attended his memorial service. Although I hadn't seen his body, and that didn't prove anything, I was sure that he was dead. My mind whirled with thoughts. It couldn't be him; it had to be his son, Charles. Mrs. Campbell had just told me that he hadn't been around. I had a good look at him just a few minutes earlier. The question wasn't why Arthur Campbell was alive but why his son was around and everyone was pretending he was at work.

My body began to stiffen in the cold. I unfolded myself from behind the tree and started to move away from the house when I realized that I was no longer holding the envelope. It was lying on the ground surrounding the tree among the faded flowers and trailing ivy that was meant to beautify the block. A small sign in the patch warned dog owners to keep their pedigreed pets away from the delicate plants.

After picking up the envelope, I remembered that my phone had vibrated just moments before. It had to be Rod returning my call. Putting the envelope under one arm, I saw that I missed two calls, I walked further down the block and listened to my messages. The first message was from Letty who wondered whether I had dinner with Rod after all. She wanted all the details if we had. The second call was from Rod.

"Daisy, something's come up. I'm not going to meet you after all. I'm with Munroe. We're at the Seventh Avenue Diner, just finishing dinner. We're just about to leave. I'll give you a call when I can."

I couldn't help but feel insecure. Rod was at the diner with Munroe. He promised to meet me for a snack after I left the Campbell house. I knew about the importance of their professional partnership and tried to let my higher thinking guide me into doing the next right thing. I learned how not to let my thoughts drag me to the edge at meetings but it was easy to forget. The last thing I wanted was an emotional hangover, with all the excitement of the last couple of weeks keeping me busy I'd been attending less meetings. If I thought in a program sort of way, I could tell myself he was in for a long night and had to have dinner. Hungry meant 'needs to eat', simple enough.

"Get it together, Daisy," I said to myself as I walked down the block dialing Rod's number. He answered on the first ring and I immediately began whispering into the phone. "Hi, it's me. You're not going to believe what I'm about to tell you."

Rod's voice was just as low. "Umm, Daisy, sorry that I can't meet up with you but like I said in the message, I'm at work."

"I totally get it. I have some news you need, both of you." I imagined Munroe sitting sullenly with her mouth puckered over a cup of black coffee.

"What news?"

"I'm on Eighth Avenue right now. Wait for me. I'll be right there." I hung up before he had a chance to answer.

The fluorescent lights were harsh at the diner. It was that evening quiet time when most families were home together. While a few single people sat at the counter, some of the booths were filled with couples talking quietly over their dinners. Munroe and Rod were at a booth. When he spotted me, he moved over, and I slid in next to him, across from the lady detective.

"I know this is not what you expected," I said. The waitress handed me a laminated menu. I might as well eat. I was hungry too. "I'll have a cup of soup. What are you serving today?"

Munroe's eyebrow cocked.

"I realize you guys are at work, but this is important. It's about your work."

"Navy bean and chicken noodle." The waitress flipped her pony tail behind her back.

"Navy bean." I thought about that and its consequences. If for some reason Rod did come over later that evening, I'd definitely regret the Navy bean soup. "Wait. Change that to chicken noodle. I'll have some crackers with that too."

Munroe must have shared my thoughts because I saw a shadow of a grin on her lips. I shrugged and kept talking.

"I saw him, you guys."

"Who?"

Of course, they wouldn't know what I'd been doing that evening. All Rod knew was that I was working late for Sophia. "Charles Campbell."

"Where did you see him?" Munroe straightened in her seat. "How long ago?"

"I saw him at his mother's house right before I came here. I had to bring some papers over there for her to sign."

"You're not going to believe this either. I saw the pixie. Her name is Sybille O'Connor. They're both at Mrs. Campbell's manor."

"You've got to be kidding." This time both Munroe and Rod looked at each other. He shifted in his seat.

"How come you didn't say anything?"

"I tried to. That's why I called you. When you called me back I was hiding from Dr. Campbell. I didn't want him to see me."

"Where was he right before you left?" Rod spoke to me but kept his eyes on Munroe as she played with the crumpled napkin next to her plate.

"He went into the garden apartment entrance of the house, but he didn't turn on any lights. You didn't ask but I'll tell you that his fiancée, Sybille O'Connor, left a couple of minutes before I did. I tried talking to her but she left in a hurry… she was in a silver Lexus, a utility."

"You know your cars?" Rod seemed skeptical.

"I do actually. As a kid, I'd name cars for my Dad whenever we were on the road. It passed the time and now it's a habit that I can't seem to get out of, no matter how much I'd like to. Know what I mean?"

Rod smiled and nodded. "I kind of did the same …"

Munroe interrupted us. "Is there anything else relevant here? Not that yours isn't a sweet story but I think you get where I'm going with this."

My mouth dropped open. This woman was just impossible and I was about to tell her that when she started up again but Rod's shark look shocked me and I closed my mouth.

"Do us a favor, Daisy, if you do see her, leave the questioning to us. Just let us know the next time it happens. We'll do the rest," Munroe ordered.

The heat rose through my body. "You know, I'm the one that spotted those two and I was the one that let you know and now, I'm supposed to butt out? Just listen to me for a second…"

"Go ahead, but hurry, we have a lot to do before this evening is over," she said drily.

"I tell you I saw Doctor Campbell's son and you don't jump up to go over there? That doesn't make sense. I know he has to be there… it's his parents' house for crying out loud."

Munroe's perfect eyebrow cocked once again. "Excuse me, Daisy, but we can't really, how do I put this, conjecture with you, know what I mean?"

"Yes, I understand perfectly. Good night." I wanted to tell her off but looking at Rod stopped me from saying another word.

The waitress was about to place the soup in front of me and the aroma made my mouth water but I wasn't going to sit and be spoken down to by Munroe. I felt my rage grow stronger, I needed to get out of the diner. My ego was getting in the way of the true intention of me telling Rod and his partner what I just saw and that was lethal.

"Daisy…" Rod extended his hand to stop me. "I'll give you a call. I promise."

I nodded. "Like I said, good night."

I walked out onto the unusually quiet street. Fall was setting in and the summer night crowd had dwindled to only a handful of people. I had to go back to my apartment where it was even quieter. I stopped to wait for the light to change and looked up at the moon. The crescent was thin and barely visible in the indigo blue sky. I realized that I was getting too involved and upset about something that really had nothing to do with me. Something had to change and that was me. I wasn't sure about what I needed to do differently but my ideas of being right in a particular situation never came to any good. Maybe I should connect with Angela or Jose. I thought about it as I crossed the street and decided to just be quiet for a while with my feelings. I'd call one of them but first I had to check in with myself. I headed up the dark block.

Munroe gazed at Rod with a glassy eyed look. "What do you make of that?" She tilted her head towards the door that had just closed behind Daisy.

"What part of 'that' do you mean?" Rod rubbed his eyes. "There's a lot going on here."

"I guess you're right. There is a lot going on and it's getting murkier. It seems as though there's something else going on that you're not talking about…"

"Well, not really…"

"Look, Detective, let me make this simple. We're a new team, yes, but my definition of team means that there is no holding back. I have to be able to trust you with my life. If I feel you're hiding something, whatever that is, my trust is going to be the size of a dried up raisin. Get it?"

He straightened his back, scratched his head, and looked at her for a long moment before responding. "I told you that it was going to take me a while to talk about the case that put me here in Yuppie-fied Brooklyn…"

"Whoa, wait a minute. We're talking about two different things here. That business, about why you were transferred, I get that. I'm not insensitive." Munroe smiled and revealed a gentleness that Rod hadn't seen in her as yet. "I'm talking about Miss Muñiz. When you two are together it's as though there's an undercurrent at play. I just want to say that out loud. She's not on the force and there's…"

"Okay…" Rod took a deep breath. "I met her at Mike's house and we clicked. We had dinner and there's something to her, I'm not exactly sure where this is going yet, but I enjoy being with her. I understand that I shouldn't be mixing business with pleasure but there's something about her that I like- a lot. She's smart. That aside, if anybody knows what's going on at Windsor, it's Daisy Muñiz. I say we listen to what she has to say."

Munroe took her wallet out, placed a few bills on the table, and shook her head. "How about I sleep on this? It's been a long day and I can't think anymore."

"Wait, what about us going to the Campbell house? We need to follow up on Charles Campbell and the woman."

She gave him a blank stare. "Why would you be going there? Really, don't you think he deserves to be there? His father is dead."

"Yes, but we still have to question him," Rod answered. "Daisy was helpful in pointing us in his direction and this is our work. I'm glad she told us that she saw him and the pixie, as she calls her. We haven't finished the job yet, Liz. We have to find out who killed Doctor Campbell and his wife. We can't stay away from them because the family is grieving." Rod sighed at the lack of reaction from his partner. "There is such a thing as being diplomatic but we still have to do our work. And, for what it's worth, I'm glad that Daisy shared the information with us."

Munroe slid out of the booth. "Just give me a night, Rodriguez, that's all I'm asking for at this point. If Charles Campbell or his fiancée have any information that would help the case tonight, they'll still have it tomorrow. Let's go."

Rod pulled a few bills out of his pocket, left them next to his plate, and followed Munroe into the cool night air.

❀

I practically slid up the stairs to my apartment. I didn't want to bump into any of my neighbors. The truth was that I didn't want to be bothered because I was so tired.

Ms. G. was licking her paws as she waited for me at the top of the stairs. I scooped her up, opened the door, and placed her on my couch. I turned on the television with the remote. I felt like I was on automatic pilot. I pressed the buttons for the classic movie channel. I didn't have to search for it. Old movies were an outlet. A commercial was on and I went into my bedroom to slip out of my clothes and put on my fluffy robe. I needed to get away from everything and I knew exactly how to make that happen.

By the time I sat on the couch, with freshly popped white kernels of popcorn filling the bowl I kept aside for evenings like this, Ms. G. had fallen asleep on one of the feathery pillows I usually laid on. I smiled as I looked at her curled up on the pillow and decided that I'd use one of the other ones. She was my night companion. I looked up at the screen and saw that Spencer Tracy was in the middle of exchanging words with Katherine Hepburn. Her red hair was glorious. Even if the film was in black and white, I knew the exact shade of her shimmering locks. I often imagined that I was her, strong, independent, and beautiful. I read in her biography that she was just as fiery as her characters in her personal life. Like me, she also watched old movies when she was in her home. Claudette Colbert, Vivian Leigh... I felt my eyes close and I drifted off into sleep.

Chapter 19

The next morning, the sun poured through my bedroom windows. I tried sinking deeper into my bed. The apartment was quiet except for Ms. G. kneading her paws on the scratchy rug I bought for her a couple of months earlier. She was making me her human in spite of me being afraid to take on that type of responsibility. I was still trying to learn how to take care of myself but she was irresistibly sweet.

I wasn't really sure how I got to bed, but not remembering the night before was nothing new. The subtle differences were that I was alone in my bed, there were no half empty booze bottles next to my bed, and I didn't have that awful feeling of shame and guilt of drinking three bottles of wine. This morning was a relief to me. Those old days were over and as long as I went to meetings and didn't pick up the first drink I'd never have to go through those terrible times again. Now, being alone was welcome. When I was still out there, being alone was something I avoided at all costs.

I looked at the clock. I stretched and got up. It had been a few days since I picked up my tarot deck. I grabbed at the first deck and quickly shuffled the cards. I fanned them out on my desk, closed my eyes, and passed my hands over them. I 'listened' through my hands for the energetic pull. My hand stopped automatically and I picked up the card that my fingers intuitively reached for. I turned it over; the knight of cups.

Rod's image filled my mind; he became my knight in shining armor riding towards me on a large white stallion. The cup was filled with love. I sighed. I was such a romantic. The wings on the figure's helmet were of

Hermes, who was also known, as Mercury, and he represented magic, wisdom, and the alchemical process. This card was perfect for me. It told me exactly what I needed to know. Getting to know Rod was magical for me. Things were moving quickly, at an almost alchemical speed. This card confirmed what I already knew, my process with Rodriguez should continue at a slow pace, the horse in the picture, seemed to be at a cantor's pace, it also held its head demurely. 'Go slow, Daisy, this is for you,' the card seemed to say, 'if you use your head and don't try to rush things.' This felt right to me. I turned the card over in my hand a few times and thought about the larger meaning. I should be attentive but not overly kooky about the whole thing. Magic was in the air and I didn't have to do anything but to be myself; that was good enough. I replaced the card in the deck and put it back in the basket with the other tarot sets.

    I took a hot shower and got ready for what I knew would be another crazy day at work. I picked a simple dark grey knit dress and paired it with my burgundy cashmere sweater. It was the softest piece of clothing I had, it was a complete splurge, and although I may not have paid it off yet, it was worth it.

    When I arrived at my office, I listened to my messages. Sophia left one saying that she wouldn't be in because she had personal business to attend to and if any essential business couldn't be put off until she returned, I should bring it to Mr. Donaldson, the C.E.O.

    I sighed when I thought about the morning after Dr. Campbell's death and my anxiety about going up to Donaldson's office. Although it all seemed a lifetime ago, it hadn't been all that long. Sophia always took the lead in most, if not all important events, and I was glad that she usually found me helpful, with 'usually' being the operative word. I hoped that nothing would require that I go to the C.E.O.'s office for help. I also hoped that Sophia was all right, it was unlikely that she would take a day off in the middle of the investigation.

The day flew by quickly with almost no interruptions. I was glad there hadn't been a need for me to contact Mr. Donaldson. Work that wasn't related to follow-ups of patients that Dr. C. and Price left behind or reports for the medical board on their work had been piling up on my desk. I was able to get almost a third down the stacks of paper, folders, and invoices that Sophia, me, had to okay. Sometimes I wondered why she gave me so much responsibility. On the day I asked her why, Sophia looked up over her lavender frames and said, "I trust you, Daisy, that's why." I was floored.

There was only one interruption that I would have welcomed- Rod's call. He didn't get back to me like he promised he would before I left the diner. I hoped he wasn't angry at me. I wished that he didn't mind that I told him what I thought could be a very important clue to the case. As my brain rattled with self-doubt, I took a deep breath. I needed to relax. Pray. Meditate. Make a meeting. Do anything but ruminate on the fact that I felt like an insecure kid when it came to Rod. This was the first chance at a real relationship since being sober. I felt as though I was fifteen years old and he was my first boyfriend. I felt myself flush when I thought of that term 'boyfriend.' The least I could do was read a copy of the Grapevine- a meeting in print. I needed some sanity and not to go off the deep end. Or even better, I thought, I could catch up with Letty when I got home.

I hurried to finish my last chosen assignment for the day and left through the emergency room exit. For some reason, the media never camped out there. I could just leave and not worry that my face was going to show up on television all over the northeast part of the country. If I was going to be at someone's house at dinner time, I wanted to be fed a nice steak or roast and not be inside of the screen on their countertops. As I walked home I could feel my stomach rumbling. I forgot to pick something up for dinner. I would have to stop at the supermarket before I got home.

❀

  Standing in front of my sink, I dried the last pan I used for my dinner of tilapia and broccoli. I caught sight of myself in the small mirror that hung on the far wall. I was surprised to see that my face was that of a composed woman, at peace in heart and mind. The truth was that I was boiling. I did the things I was supposed to keep me in balance; I cooked and ate a nutritious dinner, chatted for a few minutes with Letty until the baby started crying, and read Step Ten in my Twelve and Twelve. But I was still bothered by Rod not having called me. Seeing Charles Campbell had been an important find and, yet, I felt that both Rod and Munroe had ignored me. I needed to talk this out with another sober soul that I trusted, Jose.
  I went down the steps to his apartment and knocked on the door. As a iyawó, Jose had to be home, he wasn't allowed out after dark for his first year and he could be depended on not to take risks.
  "Hi." He opened the door a crack. I tried to see if Rubio was behind him but he was blocking the door. "What's up?"
  "Can I come in? What's up with you, acting so weird?" I pushed the door a little. "Rubio home?"
  "No." He stepped back and opened his door. "Come in."
  "Why are you acting so strange?" I asked. "If you

don't want me here, you could just say so. No need to hide behind the door."

"It's not really that," he said, shaking his head. "Sit down, I love that you decided to come down for a visit. It's me, you're right, I am a weirdo."

"Stop! What the heck is going on?" I sat down.

"I feel like a weirdo stalker. I know that I don't have much to do, no job, and so many restrictions, that when I hear you come in, I'm like a lost puppy. Haven't you noticed? It seems as though every time you walk into the house, I'm there…"

"Well, now that you mention it, I guess so. I hadn't noticed it until just now. I love you, Jose, and I don't mind having you around, if you're feeling weird about it just remember that you're almost done with the year. Before you were initiated you were always on the go, busy, meeting people, working, whatever it was that you two were doing together… where is he?"

"Rubio's at a fundraiser for the uptown gallery that Moises is trying to keep alive. People love to ooh and ah over art but buy it? Forget it! That's why Rubio is getting big financial backing. I was just making hot lemonade, want a mug?"

"Sure, sounds great. I have to talk to you about some stuff too. I'd like to get your opinion of a few things, I'm not sure if I'm overreacting."

"I'll be right out." He walked toward the kitchen. "Make yourself comfortable."

I stretched out on the couch that I spent many an evening crying on during my early sobriety. The living room was comfortably furnished with fine wood furniture. The room's understated elegance showed Jose's financial expertise integrated with Rubio's artistic background. The truth was that Rubio didn't have a care in the world when it came to money. His parents were extremely well off and Rubio made the decision to live independently, but you could tell he came from a privileged background. Rubio was often told that he had wealth in his aura. The running joke was that he may have had gold coins in his energy field but Jose had them in his pocket.

Jose came back into the living room and handed me the hot mug. I sat there sipping the steaming buttered lemonade that he made.

"I have to tell you about the craziest things that happened last night. It all had to do with the murders at the hospital, I think. Maybe I'm making too much out of it, as apparently Rod and Detective Munroe thought but…"

"Take a breath, Daisy," he suggested. "What are you talking about?"

"I saw Charles Campbell, the older son that didn't go to the memorial. He's right here in Brooklyn. I'm not really sure why…"

"Come on, his dad was just found murdered, not to mention his stepmother. Why wouldn't he be here?"

"It just seems off…"

"I think that maybe you're making too big a deal about it."

I shrugged and took another sip before I went on. "Maybe you're right but I also saw his fiancée and you know what? She's the pixie I was trying to tell everybody about. She was around the night that Doctor Campbell was killed."

"So was I…" Jose started to laugh.

"Ha ha, very funny, you know what I mean." Sometimes Jose could be annoying. "The crazy thing is… that for a moment I thought that he was the real Doctor Campbell, you know, his father. I guess that first I was in shock over seeing the pixie whose real name is Sybille

O'Connor. She seems so much like a pixie or a fairy…definitely not from this planet. She scooted out of there when she recognized me. I mean… I think she recognized me. I'm not sure. She acted like I scared her or something…"

"So, the son looks exactly like the Dad?" Jose was starting to get interested in the details. "That's saying a lot. I wonder if whoever killed Dr. Campbell was aiming for his son. Some sort of dirty business? Was he being blackmailed for something? Have you had time to think about it?"

"Not really. But mistaken identity doesn't feel right, if I go by my hunch, like Hector said to do. Why would someone come all the way up here to New York to kill Dr. Campbell's son if he lives and works in Baltimore?"

"True. To be fair, though, there's got to be a connection of some sort." He pondered for a moment. "Have you done any more meditation? Tried to get any information that way?"

"No, I just haven't had the time. I know that's the message we keep getting, meditate, meditate, but how do you fit it into the real world?"

"Close the door, close your eyes. It doesn't have to be fancy. You are all you need. Everyone thinks they have to set up with music, candles, or have a darkened room. That can't be further from the truth. I agree, that all helps to bring one to a quiet state but the trick is to learn to quiet your mind, let's say, if you're on a train or in a cab. Quieting the mind is the goal, not the beauty of your meditation spot."

"I never thought of it that way. I thought that since I finally had my own apartment that it would come easy. Nothing does. I have to put my best foot forward for everything." I sighed. "It can get kind of tiring."

"Having a monkey brain can exhaust us. Meditation helps with that too. Some of the busiest people I know carve time out for meditation."

"You're right. I have to do something to fit it in." We sat quietly for a couple of minutes and then I remembered to ask him about what was going on in his life. I was a slow learner but I was getting it. "What about your interview? Did you ever hear back from that job you interviewed for?"

"I'm having a second interview tomorrow. This time it's with the associates. That's what the job would be for, a junior associate. There will probably be about five or six people at this one."

"Aren't you nervous?" I asked. "I'd be biting my nails."

"Let's face it Daisy, you're always biting your nails," he said laughingly.

I hit him gently with a deep rust colored throw pillow from the couch. "I can't even get mad at you because it's true." I tried to hide my hands behind my back. "I won't show you but they're finally growing out a little."

"My nervous Daisy." He took one of my hands and gave it a squeeze. "I'm nervous too. I want this job so badly that I can taste it. I don't want them to smell the anxiety on me, though."

"Is there something you can do to make sure that you get the job? Have you asked Hector?"

"I would have asked him except that I think that if I'm not supposed to get it, then I don't want to force the issue. People ask for things and then live to regret it. I'll do my best and if God and Obatalá think the job is for me then I'll get it. I have no doubt about that."

"I wish I could be so full of faith. I'm lucky if I say prayers once a week."

"Don't worry about that. One day a time, you just do the best that you can. I'm wearing my grey suit though; it matches my eyes. Rubio says that I look beautiful in it."

"How are you two doing? Are things any different for you?"

"After the misa we both did a limpieza for ourselves and for the apartment. All the works of an intense spiritual cleansing, flowers, cascarilla, you name it. Everything that Hector told us and, knock-wood, we're back on track." He pretended to knock on his forehead.

"Oh, wait, I didn't tell you," I said excitedly. "I did have a meditation a couple of nights ago, I didn't count it because it wasn't planned like you said. I was waiting for the papers from Mrs. Campbell. So I sat and tried to get impressions of what was going on in there but all I saw was Rubio. He was signing some papers and was dressed in a tux."

"You're right on track. He's leasing a store front on Atlantic Avenue as a gallery. What else did you see?"

"It went well, he signed and everyone toasted. Mostly men there."

"Exactly as he said..." Jose confirmed.

"There was one female there. This probably doesn't mean anything, but I didn't like her. The way she looked, like she had something up her sleeve. Her eyes glittered."

"That's Selena Montoya. I don't like or don't trust her. I met her at dinner a couple of times. I hear that she's got a drug problem. Manteca. But you'd never know it. Not with the money she's got. Heroin sustains that woman. She's been using for years. She's married to Papo Montoya. He's, how can I put it? Well connected. Streams of money. I don't particularly like Rubio doing business with them but it's not easy to get property leases in Brooklyn."

"I don't think the woman is who you described. This one was dressed to the nines. She was beautiful. How could she be using? It had to be someone else."

"It's her. Take my word for it. That lady seems to have made a deal with the devil. That's why I'm a bit worried about Rubio dealing with them."

"He's clean though, isn't he?"

"Yeah, no worries about that. It's just bad business… it doesn't feel right to me," Jose said. "All I can do is support him and let him know when I think something's not right."

"That's where faith comes in, I guess. But getting back to Doctor C. and his son, I keep wondering and feeling like there's some connection there."

"Want to try something?"

"What do you have in mind?"

"How about we meditate together? Let's see if we can see something. Rubio and I have done it before. We can help each other out."

"Sure. What do we have to do?"

Jose got up from the couch and went over to the console table. He picked up a tray that held a large abalone shell, a bunch of white sage, and a small white candle already set in a small crystal holder. He lit the candle with a match and then broke off a tiny branch of sage and lit it. The air was quickly filled with the strong aroma. He opened a drawer in the console and pulled a red wrapped item out. He opened the fabric piece and held up a large brown and white speckled turkey feather; Jose smudged himself first and then me.

"Have meditation kit, will travel." I inhaled deeply. "This smells so good."

"Take your shoes off and sit across from me."

Doing as I was told, we touched hands lightly,

closed our eyes and, simultaneously, began to breathe in deeply. We settled into our combined meditation positions, both of us accessing our higher selves. After several minutes, in tune with each other, we both inhaled, then exhaled deeply and opened our eyes. It seemed as though the room lighting had actually changed. Everything had a much rosier glow to it.

Jose was the first to speak. "I had a few images. Would you like to share first?"

"Go ahead. I didn't see so much as felt some things."

"It was almost as though I'd gone into the dream or meditation you had a while ago," Jose explained. "The one where the two masked medical people were arguing. I could see them. There was a lot of friction there. They were arguing and seemed to be on the point of violence. One was definitely a woman. The other was tall. He had those piercing dark eyes. Did Doctor Campbell have those?"

"Yes, they were a dark blue... almost purple. It was probably Doctor Campbell, but which one is a mystery to me. Now that I've seen his son I'm not sure which is which anymore. Did you see anything else?"

"No. That was it."

"I didn't see anything but I felt a sense of urgency, like I needed to be somewhere. Like right now, I mean. As in we shouldn't be sitting here... like we should be somewhere else."

"What do you say we go to the hospital? That's where I saw the images, in the O.R. suite. The lockers were in the background."

"I could get in but what about you? It's after visiting hours." I tried to figure out a way to get Jose past security. "We could sneak you in the back somehow or I could tell them you're my friend."

"Let's just go. We'll figure it out on the way there."

Before leaving, Jose was careful to snuff out the candle.

"Obara melli," he said. "I can't leave candles burning. I have to be very careful with flame or fire of any kind. Another nifty bit of information from my itá."

"That sounds like lots of fun. Not! There are so many warnings, I don't think I could stand it, living in fear all the time."

"Not really. I take it more like being aware of what could help or hold you back," he said and shut the door behind us. We crept down the stairs. It was late and there was no point in waking Marge up. She could be counted on to hear every last sound in the house. Fortunately, she wasn't a nosy landlord.

We walked out into the night.

❀

The lights at the hospital could be seen blocks away. The building was only a few stories high to conform to the neighborhood zoning laws but since there were no other tall buildings around, it had its presence. There were always people milling about whatever time day or night. There was a difference tonight, though. The shooting of the lawyer had decreased the number of news reporters but unlike previous days the media could not be found.

"What's going on?" I asked. "Why aren't the vans here?"

"Didn't you see the news tonight? There was a bomb scare in the downtown area near the courts."

"Are you serious? This is ridiculous. I should know that…"

"You should be checking the news, Daisy. We never know what's going on these days, do we?"

"Whatever, I guess you're right. I can't keep up with everything." I scanned the area. "We should probably just walk in the front door. It'll be less suspicious that way, even though it's after visiting hours. Maybe security won't be so strict."

"Are you kidding? After a murder here, a bomb scare downtown? Daisy, wake up, sweetheart, please."

I shrugged my shoulders and smiled devilishly before we walked into the front lobby and, sure enough, security was in place behind the desk. The evening guard barely looked up as we approached the desk. He gave me a half nod but when he spotted Jose behind me he seemed to suddenly be on alert and put his hand up.

"Excuse me, sir, are you new here?" he asked without waiting for an answer. "Next time, wear your ID, please. I don't want to hassle you, okay? So make it easy on both of us, okay, doc?"

Jose's white iyawó outfit blended in nicely with the other medical personnel strolling through the corridor. No wonder the guard thought he was a doctor.

Jose nodded back at the guard. "Sorry, chief, will do."

As we ducked around the corner I couldn't help but stifle a giggle. "You a doc, really? Since when?"

"I didn't say I was a doctor… I just didn't say I wasn't." He winked. "I've got to watch the lying too."

"Not even a white lie?"

"Well… maybe a white lie, sometimes, rarely, if you know what I mean."

"I told you the rules that a person has to follow may just be too hard." Part of me was attracted but another was totally repelled. Me following rules was never easy. The best I did was at work and that was because I genuinely liked my job.

"Maybe, right now, let's go to the locker room. That's what we saw, isn't it?"

Nodding, I led the way through the fire door that led to the staircase. You could hear a pin drop. There was no one in sight. The echo of emptiness filled the staircase with a booming noise.

"Eerie, isn't it?" I whispered. "Just think, this must have been exactly like it was the night that Doctor Campbell was murdered. I hate to think of him all alone like that."

Jose stood right behind me. His expression was grim as he started to climb the stairs after me. He took a once over of the hallway. "I know this has nothing to do with the murder but there are so many spirits here. No wonder Hector told me to stay out of hospitals for the year. The air is thick. Can you feel it?"

I was surprised. "Not really. I didn't know that you weren't supposed to be here. I can't imagine you breaking rules."

"I needed to be here with you. We're buddies, aren't we?'

"Through thick and thin." I smiled back at him as my thoughts flashed to how helpful he'd been to me when Lou died. "I owe you one. In fact, I probably owe you two." I gave his arm a squeeze as we continued to the operating suite. The double doors were emblazoned with a sign warning all non-surgical personnel to stay out of the area.

I put my hand up to stop him and fished in my bag to remove my key. The O.R. automatic door could be opened without pressing the button. Being Sophia's assistant had its perks. We'd be in without anyone knowing we were entering. Because it was being opened manually, the heavy door required the effort of both Jose and me to pull it open.

We entered the dark suite. I put my finger to my lips to make sure he would stay as quiet as possible, even though I didn't think that Jose was going to say a word anyway. We crept along the corridor. It was ghastly stark and disconcertingly quiet without the hum of the machines and no clinicians anywhere around. The silence was impenetrable. There were no patients moaning or calling out for help as they sometimes did in fear or pain as they waited for their surgeries. Suddenly, I heard what seemed to be a whimper coming from the locker room area.

Frozen, afraid to move forward, not knowing what we'd see, I grabbed Jose's hand.

He pulled me to the side. "We have to find out where that came from," he whispered into my ear.

"Quick, let's go into scrub room. We can get a good look into the locker room from there. I bet that's where the noise came from."

The room was partitioned with a glass enclosure that was covered with a venetian blind. We sidled up to the window and peered through.

Charles was scowling and his face was reddened as he stood in front of the wall of lockers. He was frantic in his movements as he pulled at each handle. Sybille stood in front of him quietly pleading with him to leave. I figured she must have been the one that whimpered since her face was wet with tears.

I motioned for Jose to follow me out. Just as we made it to the outer corridor we heard the sound of banging against metal.

"Jose, just like I saw it in the vision. He's losing it," I whispered. "He's trying to open those lockers. Anything in them had to have been removed a long time ago. I don't get it."

"I don't think it's for us to get. You need to call Rod. Let's get out of here before they see us."

"You're right, let's go." I began fishing into my bag for my phone.

"It's safer to call from the outside, hurry!" Jose said as he pulled me by the arm.

We rushed out into the stairwell and were half way down the stairs when we met up face to face with Munroe. Rodriguez was right at her heels.

Munroe was the first to gain her composure. "What are you two doing here?"

"That doesn't matter right now." Jose was quick to answer. "You need to get to the lockers. Dr. Campbell's son and his fiancée are there. He's about to tear the place up."

"What are you doing here?" I asked." How did you know?"

"We went to see him at the house and the maid told us that the family was out for the evening. I guess she wasn't lying after all. Then I got the thought it would be best to follow you. I thought you two would never leave the apartment."

"Let me take you there. I know the quickest route." I pointed toward the stairwell. "Follow me... the second floor."

The glance between Rod and Munroe was so fleeting that I wasn't sure I'd actually seen it, but when they nodded I knew it was proof that these two were close. They had a partnership like no other I had seen; it was one that I didn't have to be afraid of. They were tight for a reason; it was a matter between life and death.

In a moment we were back in the scrub room. Rod jerked his thumb at us. It was obvious that he wanted us to scram but Jose and I were frozen. We could hear that they were still going at it. As Rod walked through the door, Jose and I peeked through the glass and saw that Charles Campbell had turned an even deeper shade of red. I watched as he grabbed Sybille and twisted her arm behind her back and pushed her towards the locker, her face wrinkling against the metal doors, blanching in pain.

Detective Rodriguez stepped closer to Charles and said with a firm voice, "Let her go."

Shocked to see Rodriguez, Charles's face turned quickly into an unrecognizable expression of violence that turned his face from red to a savage pale yellow, pulling Sybille towards his chest, he shielded his body with her delicate frame. With strong arms, he seemed to almost crush the poor girl as he tightened his grip around her chest, handling her like a ragdoll.

"What do you think I am? Stupid?" He screeched like an angry adolescent, as his voice pitched higher. It was obvious that he wasn't in control of his actions and that his mind had cracked just like his voice.

"We can talk about this," Rod cajoled. "There's no harm done here, Doctor."

"Oh, is that what you think?" Charles's voice became even shriller. He had checked out of reality. "You're all alike... just like him." He reached into his pocket with his free hand and pulled out a scalpel and held it to his fiancée's throat. "Do you think I don't know what you're thinking? That I haven't known what you're thinking?"

There were beads of perspiration on his and Sybille's foreheads. Her body went limp.

"Let her go, Charles," Rodriguez commanded. "Just let her go."

"No, I'm not an idiot." Charles had difficulty holding her up. She was in a dead faint.

Suddenly, Detective Munroe came through the main door to the locker room. She was close enough to touch him if she were to reach out. Holding her gun with both of her hands, she pointed it straight at his head.

"Drop the scalpel and the lady."

In the millimeter of the second that he hesitated, Munroe clocked the gun. The sound of the barrel clicking made me jump back into one of the steel shelving systems. A pile of autoclaved trays scattered to the floor. The sound reverberated in the room.

Charles turned slightly to see where the noise came from. As his head swiveled, Munroe pressed her gun to his temple causing him to raise his arms releasing everything. Sybille crumpled to the ground and the scalpel pinged as it hit the floor. He fell to his knees and began crying into his hands. No longer a grown male or adolescent, he quivered like a tiny bird.

This behavior was almost more frightening than how he had acted just a moment ago. I grabbed onto Jose's arm. "What gives? I don't think he's all there."

"You and me both…"

Rodriguez hurried over to the young doctor and pulled him up, cuffing him in one fell swoop. Charles wiped his runny nose on his shoulder as he sniveled.

Munroe unhooked her radio from her belt and called for backup to get Charles to the precinct and for emergency medical assistance for Sybille. She still lay on the floor but was beginning to move her legs.

"I don't want to take any chances with this lunatic," Munroe said as she gave Charles a strange look. "One minute he's a raging bull threatening to kill his girlfriend and the next minute he's an infant."

"I wouldn't worry about this guy. I'm not about to let him go anywhere," Rod said as he secured the handcuffs. "He's got some explaining to do... why he's here in a restricted area and what he's doing trying to get into the lockers. Crazy but not that crazy. What's that old saying? Crazy..."

I finished the sentence for him. "Like a fox."

Chapter 20

It had been an accomplishment, being able to get everything in order to celebrate my first year of sobriety. My living room was crowded with friends who came to share in my happiness. Some of the guests crammed together on the sofa and others were perched wherever they could find a sliver of space. I closed my eyes for a minute relishing my luck. Before I'd gotten sober I never had such a large group of people in my house. Everyone seemed to be having a good time but I couldn't help remembering my many lonely evenings in that living room. My mind was haunted by the night I'd fallen with the cocktail glass in my hand. I cut my hand and the bleeding wouldn't stop and I had to knock on Jose's door for help. That was the first time he tried to 'Twelve Step' me and it had gone in through one ear and out the other but the seed was planted. Now we were celebrating my one year anniversary. Sober.

"I've got to hand it to you," Jose said. "You did great this year, Daisy."

The dismal images quickly faded and I couldn't stop smiling. I was so proud. Sure, pride was one of the seven deadly sins that Angela told me I needed to work on but for today it was all right to bask in my glory. Angela was talking with one of the other regulars from our home group meeting. Even Marge, who sat on one of the chairs like a princess, was moving to the beat of the music. Jose had insisted on helping her up the stairs to my place. I was to glad to have Marge here to celebrate the moment with me.

"Thanks, I'll say it again; I owe it all to you." I gave my best friend a hug. "I didn't even realize I had a problem and now I have a solution."

"The good news is that there's always a solution," he said. "I have more good news…"

"Really?" I was eager to hear it. "What is it?"

"The job," he said. "They hired me. I start the second Monday of the month."

"Do you think it's because you wore a suit?"

"Who knows? I'd like to think it was because of my qualifications and they got to see me for who I am and not my whites, but I guess I'll never know."

"Are you going to stop wearing your whites? Don't you have a couple of more months to end your year?"

"No," he said. "I'm not going to stop wearing white entirely. I'll wear regular clothes to work and I'll change into my whites when I get home. Plenty of people do it. I have to eat and pay my rent… 'First things first'."

I loved how practical he was being. The program slogans helped out in every situation. "I'm so happy for you about the job. Congratulations! Rubio must be thrilled."

"He is." I could swear that Jose actually blushed. "He'll be here in a few minutes. He had to stop at the gallery to pick up some documents and blueprints."

"I guess I should say congratulations to both of you. Things are looking up, aren't they?"

We stood together basking in our respective and collaborative happiness for a minute when Rod sauntered over to us. I felt myself blush this time as I watched him make his way through my friends. He was so good looking. I was glad that we were getting to know each other better. By the way he looked at me I knew the feeling was mutual.

I reached out as he neared me and held his hand. I felt like I was sixteen again but was glad that I wasn't.

"Hey, I'm really glad that you made it, I know that you were busy wrapping things up. Letty tells me that Mike is always up to his neck in paper work when a case is completed."

"That's true, but I wouldn't miss your celebration." He smiled at me. "You look great."

"Thank you," I said. We stood closely together. It seemed like the rest of the room had dimmed. I was entirely focused on him; the smell of his aftershave brought me back to the night of the misa. I could still feel his kiss…

"Earth to Daisy," Jose's voice brought me back to the room. "Are you in there?"

"Very funny," I said. I knew that he was right; I had a house full of people here that I had to concentrate on.

Jose turned to Rod and immediately began asking questions. "What I want to know is how the statement went. We only know that Charles was arrested for the murder of his father and his stepmother. Did he give a motive?"

Rod turned so that his back was toward most of the others. Because he faced the sound bar his words weren't carried to anyone nearby. "He did. He confessed easily… almost too easily. It was as though he couldn't wait to get caught. The whole thing was insane."

"Do tell," Jose encouraged.

"Charles had a major beef with his Dad, the womanizer."

I caught my breath. "But murder? His own father?"

"It seems Charles was engaged to Gloria Price when they were interns."

"What?" I asked. "This is crazy. How come I didn't know this?"

"Not many people did. Somehow they managed to keep that quiet." Rod seemed pensive for a moment. "Apparently, around the time of the wedding Dad cut Charles out of the will. Price insisted on it."

"That was the motive? That's ridiculous. He also killed Price because of the money?"

"When Charles was in the back of the car he kept repeating, she laughed in my face, she laughed in my face. You have to remember the guy was incoherent. There's stuff that's not going to come out until the hearing."

"He gets a hearing even though he confessed?"

"You bet he will. I'm sure that his mother will hire the best defense attorney; he is the first heir to not only the Campbell fortune but also to her lineage. Mrs. Campbell's maiden name is Fitzgerald; apparently she comes from a very powerful family. She's going to make sure Charles doesn't go down so easily."

Rod stopped speaking just as I noticed that Allie was standing by the door.

"Sorry, guys, I'd love to hear more but Allie just walked in and I'd like to welcome her. Promise me that you won't say anything more until I come back."

I squeezed Rod's hand. I hated to leave him for even a minute but Allie looked sort of pale standing by herself. I crossed over to her and gave her a big hug.

"I'm glad that you could make it," I said. "I was a little afraid that you wouldn't want to come over, you know, some of the other nurses are here... should I shut up now? Am I making things worse?"

"No. It's okay. We're okay with the company." Allie patted her still flat belly as she smiled at my verbal clumsiness. "Well, it's all over isn't it?"

"Yeah, I guess you could say that." I didn't want to go into what Rod had just been talking about.

"I got good news," Allie said. "Human Resources called me. They told me that my position was still open if I was interested in coming back."

"And?" I couldn't help but think that would be a

pretty challenging thing to do given the circumstances.

Allie nodded. "I'd better get back to work. I have two of us to take care of now. The medical insurance is absolutely necessary but, mostly, I love my job."

"I'm happy for you." I gave her a quick hug. "Can I ask you something about 'you know what'?"

She breathed a deep sigh. "You might as well… I can practice my answers on you. I'd rather the truth be out there rather than the gossip that I'm sure will happen."

Allie tilted her head to a corner of the living room where two of the Recovery Room nurses stood. They seemed deep in conversation and Amy, the younger one, kept looking over her shoulder at us.

"Don't pay attention to that," I said, waving my hand. "Besides, you can't be sure that they're talking about you." I took a minute to gather my thoughts and come up with my real question. "You said that Doctor C. knew that you were pregnant. What about that? I mean, legally, of course."

"I don't know. I have time to figure out what I'm going to do. No more impulsive moves. I want to do what's right for me and the baby. If I decide to do anything it would have to be after the baby's born anyway. I figured that I need DNA proof."

"Can't you get an amnio?"

"Why would I do that? That isn't exactly the safest procedure."

I couldn't help myself; I had to ask her what really was on my mind. "Allie, we're all adults in this room. What I mean is… well… Dr. Campbell wasn't known for having the most integrity and I was thinking of your health and the baby's, if you know what I'm trying to say…"

If you're wondering whether I have an STD, I'll clear that up for you right now." She flipped her long hair behind her shoulders. "I got examined and had all the tests I needed completed as soon as I suspected I was pregnant. My baby and I are okay, we're okay."

Even though her words were said with a bit of edge, her face looked soft and as if she were about to cry.

"I just care about you, that's all, about both of you," I said. "That's it and I mean that. I'm here for you, we're friends."

Allie took my hand, gave it a quick squeeze, and then abruptly changed the subject. "Something smells really good in here. What's for dinner?"

"Food will be ready in a minute. In the meantime, let me introduce you to some folks. I want you to relax and enjoy yourself."

"No sense in feeling sorry for myself? Is there?" Allie looked around the room filled with people.

At that moment, Hector came out of the kitchen and waved a towel for everyone's attention. "Okay, everyone, the pernil is ready. All I need is a little help in serving."

"I think that's my cue." Allie walked over in his direction. "Best I keep busy."

Jose sidled over to me and whispered in my ear. "She doesn't look too happy, does she?"

"She's all right. Allie's not a victim. She's a survivor. You'll see."

"I hope. She seems like a nice girl, a bit trusting… but okay. Well, here comes your beau."

I gave Jose a sidelong glance. "My beau? I like the sound of that. My beau."

Rod stood at my side. "I like that, too. Your beau."

I felt something tickling my ankle and looked down to see Ms. G. purring her way into the celebration. I picked her up and felt her strong purr vibrate on my arm. "She sleeps with me at night. Sweet, huh?"

"Yes, sweet."

I searched out Rod's hand again and held it. It was warm and felt just right in mine. Today marked a year that I hadn't picked up booze. While my program wasn't perfect, I had a roomful of friends, I was on speaking terms with at least my father again, and I wasn't in jeopardy of losing my job or my mind. The idea of a spiritual life was more reality than just thinking about what I didn't have. Hector and I were busy planning for me to receive my collares soon. I couldn't remember the last time things in my life were working so well and I wanted to keep it that way. One day at a time.

A few days later, I sat next to Sophia in the dining area of my apartment. I had to admit to myself that watching her try my new shrimp gumbo recipe was nerve wracking. I hoped that she would say yes to my invitation but I felt a little shy now that she was sitting at my dining table. Our friendship was deepening. Sophia was a sort of mentor to me; she was someone that I looked up to and could depend on, someone that had that wisdom that I craved. She stayed in my corner from the days I crawled in late to work to our most recent partnering on the Campbell family tragedy. Despite the fact that she disagreed with some of my opinions she never set out to hurt me in anyway and that all meant a lot to me.

"So, what do you think?" I could barely contain my anxiety. "I made it once and I liked it but…"

"Daisy, I had no idea that you were so talented in the cooking department. This is delicious." She dabbed at her lips with a cloth napkin. I made it a point to set the table in the most elegant way with items I had stored in my linen closet that almost never saw the light of day.

"Do you entertain regularly, dear?"

I was about to say no, but then I thought about it and realized that I actually did. Over recent weeks, I had invited Allie, Jose, Hector, and all of my friends who had come to my party. Angela spent a few evenings over too but that wasn't really entertaining. She helped me with my 'Fourth Step' and outlined it for me the old fashioned way- right out of the Big Book.

"I guess I do," I answered. "This is all new. I wasn't really inviting people over when I was still living with Lou..."

Sophia interrupted me by clearing her throat. She put her hand up to stop me and then sipped at the glass of water. "Let's not go down that road, dear. You've most certainly changed paths."

I nodded, gratefully. She was right to stop me from going on about the woes of what I now saw as a past life. "You're right, of course." The awful sequence of events regarding the Campbell family was over and it seemed my ingrained way of thinking negatively was about to jettison me into yet another dark area. I needed to remember that and list it on my Fourth Step list of character defects. Those could be changed into strengths, according to Angela.

Sophia continued. "I must say that this whole affair has changed me in a way that I certainly couldn't foresee."

"How do you mean?" I was surprised to hear her say that.

She seemed thoughtful as she ate more of the savory shrimp. "As the Administrator, I was privy to information that I chose to ignore. Price's behaviors, as well as Arthur's, were beyond unacceptable. The push from above reminding me that the hospital is a money making venture was the excuse I used all too readily to keep them on staff. I received many complaints and basically sat there with my hands folded."

"Are you blaming yourself?" I was embarrassed to hear this confessional from Sophia. I had also taken the time to introspect about how I might have done things differently and also on what I would have continued to do. "Because if you are, you have to know that none of it was your fault. There was a lot at a stake for everyone involved."

"Well, I never ignored any of the sexual harassment charges. Those we took care of... but knowing the caliber of indecency that poured from that man should have been a sign that the hospital and the patients deserved better."

"Now, I think it's my turn to stop you." I put my hand on her arm. "You could never have known where this would all lead, you just couldn't."

"Charlotte has been my friend for years. I knew so much of the inner dealings of that man. She entrusted me with some of her deepest thoughts and feelings. I had a hard time separating that out from my duties when I sat at my desk at work."

I nodded. I could see how it could all become murky.

"Charles is going to be away for many years. You do know that he's in a maximum forensic security institution."

"I didn't know."

"Ted not only lost his father but his brother as well," she said softly as she pushed her plate away. Although she was serious, I noticed that she practically cleaned the plate. The dish must have been good to have made it through such a heavy conversation. I don't know why I thought that she only told me she liked it to placate me. I still had so much to work through. "There's more..."

"How do you mean?"

"It seems that the will had never been changed after all. Charles was still slated to inherit half of his father's estate upon his death... the other half is going to Ted when he comes of age. Charles won't be seeing it until he's released. When that will be, I have no idea. Although he's confessed, he still has to return to court for his sentencing."

I tried to assimilate everything Sophia was saying. "So you mean, two people are dead for no reason... no reason at all?"

"It's all complicated but I do believe that Charles let his thinking get the better of him. I can't even begin to figure him out from an emotional standpoint. It will be good for him to be away. He's a hurt and very dangerous man."

"Yes," I agreed. "I hope that Ted will get the help he needs to work through all of this."

"I'm certain that Charlotte will spare no expense for her son."

I nodded but couldn't help to think of Mrs. Stills who had experienced a tragedy of another kind. The fact her parents were well off had no bearing on the help she should have, but never received in order to deal with her pain. It took almost a lifetime before she sought help on her own. Maybe it would be different for Ted.

"I don't know how Charles could have murdered his father, Sophia!" I heard myself blurt out.

"Apparently, Charles originally didn't mind when his father moved in on Price. She was a handful."

"But where does Sybille O'Connor come in? Is she really his fiancée or is that not true?"

"Yes, she was, that's a definite. Seems he paired up with her almost immediately after the breakup. She's a nurse he worked with and apparently knew what was going on. I think her mothering personality helped her believe that she might save him."

"He was a surgeon. They're a special breed, not afraid of a little bloodshed."

"That may be true, but the difference is that they're usually on the other end of the life-death cycle. They're supposed to save lives, not take them, Daisy."

"I know, you're right, I don't know what I was thinking." I sipped at my iced tea. "But I do wonder what put him over the edge? I guess ultimately he couldn't deal with the fact that his father was marrying his ex."

"Gloria Price had a way with people."

"I'm almost afraid to ask... what did she do?"

"It seems that at the wedding reception she laughed in Charles' face. She told him that Arthur had the will redone right before the wedding. Mocked him. In the event that his father died everything would go to her. Price wouldn't have it any other way."

"What did she have on him? Why would Doctor C. write his sons out of his will? Blood is thicker than anything else. He loved his sons. I know that. Have you ever seen him with Ted? Every day was 'take your son to work day' for him."

"Apparently, she'd gotten wind of some pretty sketchy behaviors of his that happened years ago." She looked at me grimly. "Rape."

Mrs. Still's image was clear in my mind's eye. I was sure that she wasn't the only one who had suffered at his hands. But there were still some parts of the puzzle that I couldn't fit together.

"But why did he end up killing Price?" I was confused. "A crime of passion is one thing but how could he still be in a rage days later?"

"He had apparently gone to the manor looking for the will. He was going crazy for it. She let him in, either not realizing he was the murderer or maybe she decided to take another opportunity to taunt him. She wasn't easy, in fact, she was a very calculated person but it seems her formula was a bit too off to save her. It seems she didn't have the will either. Arthur, in his obsessive-compulsive way, had hidden it. Charles went crazy looking for it in the doctor's home. Gloria didn't know where he'd hidden it, either."

"Was that what he was looking for at the hospital?" The situation was beginning to clear up for me. "The will? He was looking for it in the locker room?

Sophia shook her head. "It seems that rage makes people do things they would never think of doing at any other time. The will was found eventually. Unfortunately, two people are dead."

"Where was it?"

"At Charlotte Campbell's manor," she said. "The will was there in the family strongbox all along."

"Arthur Campbell kept his will at his ex-wife's house?"

"Those two loved each other. She couldn't tolerate his way with women but stayed close to him in every other way."

"Just as it was making sense, I'm totally confused again," I said.

"Love is like that sometimes. I think money was a factor but remember she was born wealthy. Her sons were her life."

I thought about my parents and how they never really got along but also stayed in each other's lives forever. They probably never considered divorce.

"So when did they find the will?" I asked.

"Charlotte disclosed that information immediately upon Charles's arrest. She thought that information would help strengthen his insanity plea."

I almost told Sophia that idea sounded just as insane but held back. 'Restraint in tongue' was needed here. Sophia and Charlotte Campbell were close, almost like sisters, and I wanted to keep neutral in this very crazy situation. "Well, I guess love is stranger than truth…" I began.

Sophia cut me off. "Daisy, I think you mean 'truth is stranger than fiction'."

I shook my head. "Good thing I have you here to keep me on the straight and narrow."

Sophia laughed. "You're learning how to do that all by yourself, my dear."

❀ ❀ ❀

It had been almost a month since the night of Charles Campbell's arrest; I stood in my bedroom and looked into my gilded mirror. My eyes were clear. They were actually vibrant. I wore my oldest and softest corduroy jeans. The fabric of my velvet shirt was luxurious but it showed several worn spots. I had these clothes for years and could never seem to part with them whenever I gathered items to donate away to people who needed them more than I did. Today, I would. I'd give them away as I released the parts of me that I no longer needed to sustain. I recently completed my Fourth and Fifth Steps with Angela and immediately knew that I had to trust Something Higher than myself.

Today I would receive my elekes from Hector. It would be my first step in formally developing relationships with the Orisha deities. They would protect me and I was willing to be open to a different way of life. If my dreams of Yemayá and my experiences were any indication of the love I might receive from them, then I knew this was the right path for me. I would be dressed in white for seven days. Jose reassured me that he would support me in any way that I needed. Sophia wasn't aghast, as I thought she would be, when I told her how I would dress at work. She merely smiled, nodded, and sent me to pick up a mocha latte for her.

    I turned to my newly prepared altar and lit a candle. I said a silent prayer and sat in meditation. I had the thought that all I needed was to be 'honest, open, and willing'. The rest would come as my Higher Power saw fit. I felt tranquility flow through me and I was glad that I was alive and ready to meet the rest of my life head on in the light of the new day.

Award winning Puerto Rican author, Theresa Varela, was born and raised in Brooklyn, NYC. She is the recipient of International Latino Book Awards for <u>Covering the Sun with My Hand</u> in 2015 and <u>Nights of Indigo Blue: A Daisy Muñiz Mystery</u> in 2016. Dr. Varela holds a PhD in Nursing Research and Theory Development and currently works with the mentally ill homeless population in NYC. She is a member of the National Association of Hispanic Nurses; a member of Las Comadres para las Americas and is on the Advisory Board of the Latina 50 Plus program. She is Co-Founder of La Pluma y La Tinta- a Writer's Workshop. Her blog LatinaLibations on Writing and All Things of the Spirit can be found at theresavarela.com

Made in the USA
Middletown, DE
26 October 2020